LIVING MEMORY

BOOK 1

DAVID WALTON

CONTENTS

for Maggie
fellow avian dinosaur watcher

CHAPTER ONE

Khorat Plateau, Northeast Thailand

The dinosaur looked more like a squashed chicken than like the fanged killers of the American movies. A curled confusion of claws and feathers and bones, its fossilized features protruded from the rock at odd angles, making its original form difficult to discern. Pakasit Paknikorn had no idea what kind of dinosaur it was, and he didn't care. Pak was a farmer, not a paleontologist. All he cared about was how much money it was worth.

Pak hefted his pickaxe. "Cut around the edges," he told his brother-in-law, Nikorn. "Get in close, or it'll be too big to lift."

"Why don't you just tell those scientists from the museum?" Nikorn said. "They'd pay us for it, and we wouldn't have to dig it out ourselves."

"Idiot," Pak said. "Ukrit will give us a hundred times what those museum people would give." Black market dealers smuggled fossils out of Thailand to foreign collectors, who apparently had a lot more money than paleontologists. And in recent months, men like Ukrit had been offering double or even triple what they had even the year before.

Nikorn made a tentative tap with his pickaxe. "This is going to take all night. What about the Americans in the village? I bet they'd pay. Americans are rich."

Pak slapped the back of his head, a little harder than he'd meant to, but that was okay. Nikorn needed a slap now and then. "Just get to work, will you?"

Nikorn sighed and raised the pickaxe over his head. He slammed it down just to the right of the embedded dinosaur. A chip of stone skittered down the slope.

"Careful, don't break it!" Pak said. "If you damage it, it won't be worth as much."

Pak made a more careful stroke on the left side. If he'd thought he could move it on his own, he wouldn't have brought Nikorn in on the secret at all. Pak had made the find all by himself. He'd gone way out past the edge of the cassava fields, where the ground turned steeply up into the hills, to cut a path so that more water would flow down the slope to his crop instead of the nearby fields. He'd done it at night, so his neighbors wouldn't see. The drought had been so severe this year that they were all desperate to claim as much of the scant rainfall as they could. But when he uncovered what looked like a tailbone with the imprint of a plume of feathers still visible around it, he knew he'd found something even more valuable than water.

Dinosaur bones had brought a lot of foreigners to Kalasin province in recent years. When Pak was a boy, he'd only seen a white European once, when a missionary woman had come to the next village over. Now, during the dry season, whole teams of foreigners set up tent camps and went fossil hunting on the plateau. Apparently this arid, rocky land had once been a lush valley where thousands of dinosaurs had lived. Or at least where they had died.

Pak returned to his find every night for a week, cutting his way into the rock by the light of an oil lamp, revealing the dinosaur little by little. The problem was, chiseling out a man-sized dinosaur made for an awfully large block of stone. There was no way he could haul it up onto the bed of his pickup by himself. He'd had no choice but to bring somebody else in to help. And while Nikorn was something of a fool, he was also family. He wouldn't betray Pak's trust, and he would do the work, even if he grumbled about it.

The temperature dropped low on February nights, but by midnight, both of them were sweating and covered in fine dust. They'd cut a channel all around the fossil and now had the more difficult job of cutting underneath to free it from the hillside.

"Maybe we should just come back tomorrow night and finish it then," Nikorn said, wiping sweat from his forehead.

Pak was too tired to smack him again. "If we leave it like this, somebody else might find it during the day," he said. "Then we'd get nothing."

"Nobody comes here. Who's going to find it?"

"When I told Ukrit what I'd found, he said he'd give us a million baht for it, if it's in good condition. A million! Think of what you could buy Boonsri with all that money." Boonsri was Pak's sister and Nikorn's wife. She had a weakness for pretty things, and Nikorn had a weakness for her.

Pak had his own reasons for wanting the money. His daughter Kwanjai was bright, as bright a girl as he had ever seen, but as the daughter of a rural farmer, she had little hope of receiving more than the most basic schooling. She had learned to read and write at the local *prathom*, but for any further education, she would need to travel eighty kilometers away to the district capital. She would need a school uniform and a place to stay. Pak couldn't afford any of that. Without money, Kwanjai would grow up making baskets and silk like her mother and never seeing the world outside of their village. A fine enough life, but he knew she could be so much more.

Cutting underneath the block turned out to be a lot harder than Pak anticipated. There was no way to take a full swing with the pickaxe. Two hours later, a central column of rock still connected the block to the rest of the hillside. Nikorn settled into a continuous complaining monologue, which Pak had long since tuned out. He took another swing at the rock, cursing. Even once they got the block free, they would have to slide and wrestle the thing a few hundred meters across rough ground to where he'd parked his pickup. He hoped they finished before sunrise.

Pak started to imagine he saw the dinosaur moving. He knew it was just a skeleton, and not even that—just the impressions of bones left in the rock long, long ago. Gleaming in the light of the oil lamp, however, the bones seemed to dance in the flickering shadows. Pak breathed in dust and coughed as dirty sweat ran into his eyes. Ukrit better not have lied to him about the million baht.

"Do you think they will bring it back to life?" Nikorn asked.

"What?" Pak looked up at him, startled at the question. "You mean like in those movies? Don't be an idiot."

"I mean like in Massachusetts. I read that they brought a woolly mammoth back to life in Massachusetts. Is that in the United States?"

"Of course it is," Pak said, though to be honest, he had very little idea of where Massachusetts was. He remembered something about a woolly mammoth being born, though. It was like a big hairy elephant that was extinct—only now, apparently, it wasn't.

As he struck at the rock yet again, Pak felt the block shift. "Watch out!"

They scrambled out of the trench they'd dug around the dinosaur. With a crack, the block broke free. Angled against the hillside, it slid forward, hit the edge of the trench, and started to roll over. "Catch it!" Pak shouted, but it was heavier than both of them put together. There was no stopping it. It rolled once and then slid down the slope, picking up speed until it struck a boulder and crashed to a halt.

Pak and Nikorn scrambled down after it, Pak carrying the oil lamp. The block was face down now, hiding the dinosaur from view. Pak prayed it hadn't been damaged by the fall. Nikorn pulled a tiny LED flashlight out of his pocket and shone it on the block. No damage that Pak could see. They couldn't slide it to the truck like this, though; the fossil would be worn down to nothing. "Got to flip it over," Pak said.

They lifted one side together, straining at the weight, until they heaved it up on its side. "Careful, now," Pak said, but too late. The uneven block kept turning, so that instead of gently lowering it, it slipped from their fingers and slammed down hard. A thin section of what Pak guessed was vertebrae sheared off and fell to the ground. Pak cursed and picked it up, wondering how many baht had just fallen off their prize.

He slipped it into his pocket. "We'll just tell Ukrit we found it that way," he said.

Nikorn reached out to touch the dinosaur's skull, just visible as a bump on the surface. It was a gentle touch, almost a caress, but instantly a fine network of cracks radiated out from the spot. Nikorn jerked his hand away.

"What did you do?" Pak shouted.

"Nothing! I just touched it!"

Pak watched, horrified, as the cracks spread, racing through the stone like shattering glass, accompanied by a sound like corn popping over a fire. When they stopped, Pak peered at the fossil. It looked much the same as it had before, only split in places with hairline fractures. Maybe it would still be okay.

A strange smell caught Pak's attention, and he noticed a fine mist drifting up from the stone. It smelled sweet and vinegary, like a fresh durian fruit. That was odd. A cold shiver passed through him. The night was getting cooler.

"Almost there," Pak said. "Let's get this thing on the truck."

They wrestled it meter by meter down the slope, careful not to let it tip again. Both of them were strong from daily manual labor, but it taxed their endurance all the same. Finally, they reached the outcropping where Pak had parked his pickup. He had backed the truck against the hillside, allowing them to slide the block right into the cargo bed from the hill. He was glad he'd thought of that—if they'd had to lift it, they might not have managed.

Pak threw a tarp over their treasure and tossed their pickaxes in the cargo bed next to it. Time to hit the road. Not that there was much of a road where they were headed.

"Where are you going?" Nikorn asked as Pak pulled the truck away from the hillside and headed west.

"To Ukrit's. This way's quicker." The straightest path was across the foothills of the mountain range that marked the northern edge of Kalasin. Pak's truck could handle the terrain, and he didn't want to take the time to go around, or risk being seen by any nosy neighbors. He drove carefully, though, not wanting to bounce their precious cargo.

The moon rose over the mountains, giving him a clear view of the way ahead. They would make the trade, get paid, and be back home before their wives woke to start preparing the day's meals. Pak could already picture Kwanjai in her smart school uniform, learning English and mathematics and making a life for herself in the wider world. Pak would miss her, but he would be glad knowing he was providing for her future.

He caught a whiff of that durian smell again. Some kind of gas, he guessed, trapped in the rock for millions of years. It made him nervous. It wasn't poisonous, was it? Or flammable?

"Hurry," Nikorn said, fear evident in his voice.

"Why? Did you see something?"

"Just hurry, okay?"

The truck hit something, bouncing over it with a jarring bang. Nikorn shouted, jerking back from the window. Pak stepped on the brakes, wondering what he had hit. Something hidden in the brush that he hadn't noticed?

"Don't stop!" Nikorn said. "Drive!"

Pak didn't understand, but he heard the near panic in Nikorn's voice, and he was starting to feel that way himself. Something was wrong here that he didn't understand. He pressed the accelerator. The pickup jolted over a few bumps and then came to a halt, wheels spinning. Pak threw it into reverse and tried to back up, but the engine just whined. They were stuck.

Pak's heart hammered. Had he run into an ambush? But what kind of thieves set an ambush in the middle of the night on a barren stretch of terrain? Had he stumbled upon some kind of smugglers route? There were regions of Thailand controlled by gangs of smugglers and sex traffickers, but those were in the jungles, and closer to the border, not out here on the plateau.

He clambered out. Some fallen tree branches that he hadn't seen in the dark lay snarled underneath the truck. Nikorn climbed out the other side. Pak examined the barrier by moonlight. Two of the thickest branches blocked the rear wheels; if they could slide them out, maybe the truck could back up and they could go around a different way.

"Come on," he called to Nikorn. "Get that side and help me..." He trailed off as he saw a gigantic brown bird standing on the rocky outcropping, looking down at him. It was the largest bird Pak had ever seen, at least as tall as his chest. The bird sidestepped lightly on taloned feet and cocked its plumed head at him.

Only, it wasn't a bird, not exactly. For one thing, its feathers were more like little spines sticking out along the top of its body and tail, shades of brown rippling as the breeze ruffled them. For another, it had teeth. Long and slender ones, like railroad spikes, but slightly curved, filling a long jaw topped with a bright, bare red patch. Pak had lived here all his life, and he'd never seen a bird like that.

This was no time to gawk at wildlife, though. They had to free the truck and make it to Ukrit's before first light. Pak called to Nikorn, who didn't answer.

The durian smell was very strong now. Pak felt suddenly afraid for the cargo. Had the jolt damaged it? He ran around to the back and threw the tarp off of the stone block. A rush of the sweet aroma washed over him, gagging him. Green liquid bubbled up out of the cracks in the fossil.

He whirled to see the bird-creature, who had impossibly appeared on the other side of the road, stepping from one foot to the other and bobbing rhythmically. Pak called for Nikorn again. Fear swelled in his chest, intensifying to a pure animal terror that paralyzed his muscles and squeezed his lungs. He couldn't breathe. His bladder let loose, and warm urine ran down his leg. He wanted to leave the fossil and run as fast as he could away from that place, but the smell, still sweet but now shockingly acrid, prevented him.

The creature angled its head, staring with unreadable yellow eyes. As unobtrusively as he could, Pak reached into the truck bed and pulled out his shotgun. He took one step back and pumped it to chamber a round. The creature opened its mouth and screeched, a bone-jarring sound that drove a wedge of pain deep into Pak's ears. Its teeth looked very sharp.

The air around him looked different, felt different. He realized he couldn't see the truck anymore. He couldn't see Nikorn. What was happening?

He raised the gun. Quick as lightning, the creature lunged, as agile as a sparrow but with the jaws of a crocodile. A scream rose to Pak's throat, but it stuck there, choking him. All he could manage was a high keening that seemed to come from the center of his soul. He fumbled with the gun, aimed it, and fired directly into the creature's face.

The thunder of the gun's report echoed back from the hills. Dazed, Pak looked around, ready to fire again. The truck was back. The creature had vanished. Nikorn lay on the ground, clutching his chest. Blood pumped over his hands and soaked into his shirt. Horrified, Pak ran to his side, seeing the shotgun pellet holes in his brother-in-law's body, but unable to process them. The creature? Where was the creature?

Nikorn's mouth moved, but no sound came out. His eyes stared at Pak, full of accusation and betrayal.

"I didn't!" Pak said. "I didn't mean...!"

He whirled around, looking for the bird-thing that had attacked him, but there was no trace of it. Not a single feather. Not even any birdlike footprints in the dust.

He looked back at Nikorn, whose eyes had gone glazed and distant. There was no saving him. But he could still save himself.

Pak ran to the truck and jumped inside, tossing his shotgun into the passenger seat. He slammed his foot down on the accelerator. The truck revved and lurched, surging forward over the tree branches. In the back, the fossil slid with a scrape of stone against metal and tumbled out of the open truck bed onto the ground. Pak didn't stop. There was no way he could get it back onto the truck by himself anyway, and he didn't want to stay here a moment longer than he had to. Somehow, that fossil had killed his brother-in-law. He leaned forward against the steering wheel, his hands shaking and his heart slamming against his chest, urging the truck on as fast as it could go.

CHAPTER TWO

S amira felt like she was desecrating a holy site. For the last month, her team had painstakingly scraped and sanded and brushed their way into this rock face, exposing the beautiful maniraptoran fossil that now stood out in dark relief against the pale sandstone. It was a new species, not yet named, beautifully preserved. A career-making find. And they were taking a power saw to it.

She felt the fury build as Arun pulled the cord and the circular saw roared to life, its etched-diamond grinding blade blurring into motion. He hefted it carefully and set his feet, maneuvering the blade toward the thin vertebrae of the creature's neck. Bethany and Gabby stood nearby, their expressions grim. Arun looked to Samira for final confirmation.

This shouldn't be necessary, she thought.

"Do it," she said.

She held her phone up, recording the event. No way was she going to let this moment go undocumented, no matter how painful. People needed to see what was happening here. Politics was once again stomping all over science, and it wasn't right.

The blade screamed as it bit into the rock. Samira turned her head away, staring out at the barren hills. The Khorat Plateau was austere and beautiful, a saucer-shaped plain undulating gently from the Phu Phan mountain range towards the distant Mekong River. Seventy million years ago, it had been a swamp, the meeting place of multiple rivers, a lush and fertile breeding ground for dinosaurs. She could imagine it as it was then: the mountains sharp and young, not yet smoothed by the erosion of millennia; the rivers bringing sediment down the slope with them, ready to bury bones and preserve them in layers of rock.

The plateau stretched across a hundred and fifty thousand square kilometers of arid hills and rural farmland, most of it untouched from a paleontological point of view. It was a lot of ground to explore, made more difficult by the fact that for weeks during monsoon season, it flooded, making it ideal for growing rice, but not for mounting fossil expeditions.

They had discovered this site when Gabby, on a survey walk, noticed a tiny, worn vertebra lying on the ground. She had thought at first it was one of the larger vertebrae of a smaller animal, but it proved instead to be the tip of the creature's tail. Gradually, over the course of weeks, they excavated increasingly larger vertebrae, then the rear legs and feet. Another few weeks revealed the sternal plates, scapula coracoid, humerus, radius, ulna, and long, slender metacarpals.

Even without processing the fossil in the lab, the impressions of the creature's feathers were clearly visible, as well-preserved as any of the famous theropods from the Liaoning formations in China. Soft tissue like feathers and skin rarely survived fossilization, and even more rarely in sandstone fossils, which formed when sediment covered bodies in water. It must have died and been covered by sediment very quickly, perhaps in a flash flood.

A white pickup roared into the clearing and slid to a stop,

kicking up a cloud of dust. The driver, a small Thai man, jumped out of the open door almost before the truck stopped moving and ran towards them, waving his arms and shouting. Beth tried to intercept him, but he pulled out of her grasp and ran at Arun, who held the whirring saw.

"Kit!" Samira shouted, her voice sharp and pleading, and he stopped short. "You know this is how it has to go."

He turned slowly to face her, his expression pained. "Please don't do this."

Kit was one of the calmest people she knew, accepting almost to a fault. It was shocking to see him agitated like this. "We have to," she said. "We can't stay, and we can't leave them. This is the only way."

"It's bad science. The work should be done here."

"I know."

The blade rang as it burst free, the animal's spine neatly severed. It wasn't the cutting on its own that bothered them. Large finds often had to be cut into pieces for transport. There was no way to move a titanosaur in one piece, for instance—the skeletons alone weighed tons, and the attached rock much more. What killed her was leaving with only *part* of the animal and without a full survey of the surrounding rock strata.

The maniraptoran they had uncovered would have weighed around two hundred pounds, in life, though it would have stood only to Samira's shoulder, with a long tail held balanced behind it. At some point in its unique evolution, its fifth digit had migrated around its hand, giving it not one but *two* thumbs. Most maniraptorans were predators, requiring sharp claws to grasp and rend their prey, but some had developed the ability to eat other things. Was this species solely carnivorous? The answer would be in its skull, or more particularly, in its teeth, but they would need at least two more weeks of careful excavation even to discover if its skull remained intact.

The skull was the most fragile part of any find, prone to crushing by the tremendous forces involved in fossilization. Many otherwise complete specimens had been discovered with the skull either missing or so pulverized that it defied reassembly. Unfortunately, they wouldn't get a chance to find out. Two weeks was a luxury they could no longer afford.

Perhaps if they'd focused on this one alone, they could have removed it entirely by now. But a dozen meters to the west, they'd found a second, and a dozen meters beyond that, a third. Thinking they had plenty of time, the team had divided its efforts, working twelve-hour days in a race to extract all three before the season was over.

They hadn't anticipated a coup. Not that such things were unusual here—the government of Thailand had been overthrown and replaced at least once a decade for the last century. But despite that turnover, Thailand had always been an open country, welcoming of foreign investment and influence. Even when Samira saw the news, she hadn't expected to be deported.

The new regime, however, had given American expatriates a week to leave the country, at which time their visas would be reevaluated on a case-by-case basis. Which meant Samira and her team had only a week to pack up and go. They *might* be allowed to return, but she wasn't betting on it. The new pro-China leadership had made it clear they suspected all Americans in the country of working for the US government as infiltrators and spies.

The sun boiled overhead, baking them in a hundred-degree oven, but Samira had never minded the heat. It was a small price to pay for the treasures buried beneath this countryside. What she minded was stupid people thinking she was here for anything else but science. What did she care whether the US or China had more influence in the South China Sea? This was an international team, doing work of international importance. She wanted to find whoever was responsible and shake them around by the throat, but as usual with visas, there was no one available to shake.

How many more fossils had been buried in this hillside? It might take decades of research to find out, but it looked like a mass death event, a flood maybe, in which whole herds had died at the same time and been quickly covered over with silt. If so, many more fossils might be scattered over the surrounding kilometers. Different species, all captured like a photograph in the middle of their lives, perhaps with nests and eggs and other indicators of how they had lived and hunted and raised their young. An encyclopedia of information about the Cretaceous to be read and understood, piece by piece. But not by Samira. Not anymore.

"COME ON," she said to Kit. "Help me get the GPR down from the truck."

She climbed into the back of the pickup they had rented for the expedition and picked her way around the shovels, picks, rock hammers, chisels, knives, brushes, barrels of plaster powder, water, glue, dozens of rolls of toilet tissue, and all the other tools of their trade. Cope and Marsh perched there as well, one on a barrel and one on a shovel handle, eyeing her with a calculating glare.

Cope and Marsh were Asian crows. Village children had found them in the road, one with a broken wing, and the other refusing to leave its side. Samira had given them food and a safe place by her tent, and now they followed her everywhere. At first, she'd left them back at the village each day, but the crows had somehow managed to track her, showing up at the site thirty minutes or so after the team arrived. Eventually, she just let them ride in the truck bed to save them the trouble. It would be sad leaving them behind, but she had no choice. There was no way the US Department of Agriculture would approve the import of two wild Asian crows. She worried that they would forget how to find food themselves once she left.

"Shoo," she said, waving them off. "Go hunt for some insects or something." The crows took reluctant flight, spreading their wings just enough to settle on the ground next to the truck. "Lazy freeloaders."

At the back of the truck bed stood the ground-penetrating radar rig, an expensive new acquisition meant to help them map what they were leaving behind under the rock. She wouldn't generally have spent her resources this way—GPR rigs were expensive and the results variable—but given the circumstances, the team had more money than they had time to spend it. She wanted every scrap of information she could gather about the site before they were forced to abandon it.

Kit climbed up beside her, a bitter expression on his face. "We shouldn't be doing this," he said. "You should leave these fossils here with me."

Samira sighed. "I can't, and you know it. I have a responsibility to my investors. You don't have the skilled manpower or the lab to handle it, and even if you did, I need research to justify my grants. I can't go home with nothing to study."

"We have a lab at Sirindhorn, and I could get students to help, maybe even for free."

Kit was the only Thai native on their team, a geology professor at Nakhon Ratchasima Rajabhat University who was trying to start a paleontology program there, the first in the nation. She had met him years ago, as a student. His English had been barely comprehensible then, but now he spoke it brilliantly. More than Samira could say about her ability to speak Thai.

Ever since the announcement that they would be forced out of the country, Kit had been trying to convince her to leave the remaining grant money with him and his few students and to leave the fossils behind for him to finish excavating. She admired his national pride and desire to see Thailand's own people uncover its secrets, but it wasn't a request she could reasonably grant. It wasn't her money.

"It won't happen," she said.

He opened his mouth to respond, then closed it again. He gripped the other side of the GPR rig and nodded to her. Together they lifted it and lowered it to the ground.

SAMIRA WHEELED the device up a steep incline to a relatively flat area above and behind the dig site. The site itself was crisscrossed with twine held taut by stakes driven in the ground, dividing the area into a neat grid, and she didn't want to remove those until the rest of the job was finished.

While she worked the machine, the others would finish cutting the exposed fossils free and pack them in plaster for transport. They would also fill the excavated holes they left behind with dirt, hoping to protect the remaining fossils from the twin threats of erosion and looting. It was worth the attempt, but Samira had little hope it would work. Everyone in the region knew they were here. If the black market fossil hunters didn't have these uncovered and stolen by this time next month, she would be surprised.

The GPR rig was mounted on wheels, with a long handle like a lawnmower. The idea was to wheel it very slowly over the ground, bouncing radar down into the rock and sensing the pattern of what bounced back. Technology that had once been used to locate enemy planes as tiny blips could now be used like magic to take pictures through solid rock. As the energy bounced off of different densities of material, different amounts of it would bounce back, which could then be used to construct an image of what lay beneath them.

Most GPR "images" barely deserved the name. They featured a mash of overlapping gray waves, smooth and uniform in some places and dark and spiky in others. If you knew what you were doing, you could interpret those wave-forms to deduce the presence of objects hidden underground. It took experience and a geological understanding of the relative densities of materials to make sense of the smeared black-and-white imagery.

In the last few years, however, advances in machine learning had produced algorithms that could take the bewildering array of reflected energy waves and actually form something approximating a picture. If the technology continued to improve at the same rate, it was going to revolutionize field work. Few paleontologists used them now, but she had a feeling that was going to change in the near future, especially if the price came down.

Samira took several passes over the area, using a different radio frequency each time. Lower frequencies could penetrate deeper into the rock, but higher frequencies provided a better resolution image. Below a few meters, she could make out only the most general of features.

As she dragged the heavy device over the uneven terrain, she wondered if there was more she could have done for Kit. He was building a paleontology program up from nothing at the university. He was serious, dedicated, passionate, and unrelenting in his loyalty to his country. She had no doubt that a few decades from now, he would be seen in Thailand as the grand old master who had inspired a generation of scientists.

But what could she have done? The money for this expedition didn't belong to her to just give away, nor could she fail to bring home the specimens the university had sent her to procure. She hoped it wouldn't ruin their relationship, as they would certainly have more questions about the site once they got to work studying these fossils, and having someone here who was willing to go look and take more samples could be invaluable.

The images scrolling past on the GPR's screen showed little of interest so far. Samira finished a pass and switched to the next lowest frequency, penetrating a little deeper. As soon as the image came back, she froze.

"Beth, take a look at this," she said.

Beth stood and stretched. She wiped rock dust and sweat from her face with a cloth. "Find something?"

"I'm not sure."

She clambered up the hillside to join her. Beth had the build of a bird, tiny and lightweight, with quick and agile movements. In Ethiopia, where they'd grown up together, she'd stood out with her pale, blotchy skin and blond hair that collected static electricity like a polyester suit. Here in Thailand, although blond hair wasn't common, black skin was even less so, and at six feet tall it was Samira who tended to stand out.

Beth reached her and peered at the screen.

"Okay, tell me I'm not crazy," Samira said.

Beth gave Samira's braid a playful tug, like she'd done ever since they were kids. "Not sure I can help you with that."

"Not crazy about *this* at least," Samira revised.

The image showed two dark, roughly parallel lines, each with short protrusions at regular intervals. "They look like vertebral columns," Beth said. "Two specimens, side by side."

Samira nodded. "Straight as an arrow, too." Usually, skeletons in rock, especially the fragile bones of maniraptors, looked like they'd been caught in a press. The vertebrae on her screen, however, and the short ribs curving out from them, looked as they might have in life—more like the skeletons of animals preserved in a peat bog than those covered by sediment or lava flow.

She pushed the machine forward a little, hoping to get a slightly different angle on the bones. As she did so, the first dark line slipped to the edge of the screen and a *third* one slid into the image, parallel to the first two. At the end of the third, a slight flare that might have been the top of a skull was just barely visible.

"Is this possible?" Samira asked. She groped for some other explanation, some way in which this was a hoax or a crazy mistake. But there didn't seem to be any way someone could have affected what was buried under this unmarked rock, and the idea that anyone could have monkeyed with the GPR's embedded software for the sake of a joke seemed farfetched. It had to be real.

"Keep going," Beth said, the excitement rising in her voice.

She did. As she pushed the device slowly across the rock, a fourth line came into view, then a fifth, then a sixth. Arun and Gabby and Kit abandoned what they were doing and crowded around to watch. By the time they had swept over the whole region, they had located twenty-seven distinct skeletons, all oriented the same way, arranged in neat rows.

"I've never seen anything like it," Gabby said. "I've never *heard* of anything like it."

Gabby was the most experienced in their party, the veteran of a dozen expeditions in the fossil-rich Patagonian badlands of Argentina where she'd grown up. Her parents were both evolutionary biologists, her father a marine anatomist and plesiosaur expert and her mother the world's leading authority on the Permian-Triassic extinction event. Gabby had known more about paleontology in elementary school than some graduate students did. If she hadn't seen it, no one had.

Arun sat back on his heels, shaking his head. "How could this have happened? Is it some kind of nesting pattern? Are these females who were unwilling to leave their nests, even in the face of a volcanic eruption?"

"Come on," Samira said. "I'd say it's pretty clear. Maybe we haven't encountered anything similar in our field, but we can hardly say we haven't seen patterns like this before."

"It can't be though," Beth said.

"Why not? Do you have a better explanation?"

Arun looked back and forth between the two of them. "Well, what is it then?"

"Bodies laid out in neat rows, all facing the same way? I don't see how we could conclude anything else." Samira gave them a nervous smile tinged with awe and even a little fear. "It's a cemetery."

CHAPTER THREE

K it couldn't wait for the American team to leave. Technically, he was a member of the team, too, but he never quite felt like it. In a just world, it would have been Thai paleontologists digging up these skeletons and Thai university labs coaxing out their secrets. Kit resented, just a little, that Americans came to his country, dug treasures out of his ground, and shipped them back to American labs to study. But Thailand didn't have the resources or the expertise to do it. He was trying to change that at Nakhon Ratchasima, but they had a long way to go.

Good Buddhists were meant to give up craving for things, to accept pain and pleasure and riches and hardship with equanimity. But Kit had never been a good Buddhist. He *wanted* things. He had wanted to become a respected professor, despite the karma of his low birth, and he had done that. His papers had been published in Thai, but he longed to be published in a real international journal, in English, to gain the respect of the scientific community. He wanted to put Thailand on the map, not just as a dig site, but as a center for scholarship and scientific achievement.

This find could accomplish all of that. Kit believed he had

the power to sow the seeds of his own future. He believed in science and its inherent value to the human race. He believed that humanity could be transformed, not by accepting what was, but by striving toward a future they could create together. Yeah, not a very good Buddhist at all.

Kit let himself dream. Over two dozen fossils in the same orientation and arranged in a pattern? Samira was right; there was no way that had happened naturally. This would be the greatest discovery in the history of paleontology, right here in Thailand, in his backyard. Not only that, but with the Americans gone, the site would be his and his alone. Surely, with such a find, he could raise the vision of his country to invest in its study. And if he couldn't, there would be investment from outside. Even a Kickstarter campaign would raise a fortune, once word got out about what was hiding here.

"What are you smiling about?" Samira asked.

Kit's attention snapped back to the present. "An intelligent species," he said. "Can you imagine?"

"Whoa, let's take it slow," Samira said. "I'm not even sure I completely accept the cemetery interpretation. We've got an interesting behavior here, that's for sure. It doesn't mean they were debating epistemology and painting the Mona Lisa."

The two of them had returned to drilling out deep cylinders of rock to bring back to the States for magnetic dating purposes. Each sample took about thirty minutes to excavate, measure, and wrap in aluminum foil for shipping. It wouldn't narrow the timing down that much, but given what they'd found, Samira wanted every bit of verification she could get.

"They buried their dead," Kit said. "It means they had funeral rituals, which probably means religion. I mean, sure, elephants have graveyards and seem to grieve for their family members, but they don't bury them in neat rows. These maniraptors had a civilization."

Samira opened another roll of aluminum foil and fashioned it into a half sphere with a point on top. "Here," she said, handing it to Kit.

"What is this?"

"A hat for you. To protect your brain from the alien dinosaurs when they beam you to their spaceship."

He crumpled it and threw it at her, hurt. "You can't throw out a reasonable theory just because it will make you look foolish on Twitter."

Now it was her turn to look hurt. "A lot of animals have pretty sophisticated behaviors. It doesn't necessarily mean human-level consciousness. Maybe they just slept lined up like that, and something killed them all before they woke."

He wanted to argue the point, but he found Samira too intimidating to want to cross intellectual swords with her. She was an impressive woman who had made a career for herself across social and cultural barriers and despite racial prejudice. Sometimes, listening to her speak, he was tempted to throw caution to the wind and ask her out, but he knew he never would. The racial expectations of his own culture would make a relationship with her uncomfortable, and besides, he didn't want to tie himself to someone whose career aspirations would draw her elsewhere in the world. His place was in Thailand, and always would be.

Kit loved his country. When the rest of the world had fought and killed each other off, his people would still be there, peacefully following the teachings of the Buddha. Their cultural heritage was unique in the world. If only he could teach his people to value the rich history of this land from *before* humans had ever set foot on it. Then it would be Thais who uncovered the bones of these long-dead creatures, Thais who discovered their secrets, and Thai museums where they were displayed to the world.

Would the new government allow him to expand his work to make up for the American resources? Would there be grants to continue the digs and invest in laboratories and equipment? He hoped so, but he would have to convince them. Scientific advancement was rarely the priority of a new regime. Without money and support, he would have trouble even keeping the looters away, never mind properly continuing the work.

"If they had a civilization, where's the evidence?" Samira continued. "Where are the buildings? The pottery? The tools?"

"The oldest pottery anyone has found is from twenty thousand years ago," Kit said. "This is at least sixty-six *million* years old. Even pottery doesn't last that long."

"There should be something. Stone foundations, at least, or artwork, or the fossilized impressions of objects they made. I can't believe there was a whole civilization on Earth before us that left no evidence of itself whatsoever."

"They might not have built buildings with foundations, or created things able to last that long. Grasses evolved late in the Cretaceous, which could have paved the way for the development of agriculture. I'm imagining an agrarian society here."

"Agrarian?" Samira laughed. "They didn't have rice or wheat in the Cretaceous. Besides, they're carnivores. These things weren't eating grass."

"Maybe," Kit said. "We don't have the skull to prove it. But even carnivores could plant to feed their herds. Think about pack animals like velociraptors following a herd, culling the old and sick, but protecting them from other predators. As they get more sophisticated, they learn to corral their herd in a canyon for the night, or lead it to fresh grass. Then they start planting fresh grass on purpose to fatten them and keep them in one place."

"It's possible," Samira said. "I just think we're getting way ahead of the evidence." A pained expression passed over her face and she clenched her fists. "If only..."

She didn't have to finish. He knew what she meant. *If only General Wattana could have waited another few months for his coup.*

Of course the Americans thought that. It wasn't their country. They probably liked having a pro-American government in Thailand, if they even thought about it at all. But with tensions in the South China Sea increasing between China and the US, the Southeast Asian countries were being forced to take sides. The US was offering trade agreements and military hardware to any potential ally in the region to let them stage planes and troops, and the old regime had been giving in to the pressure. Wattana didn't want Thailand to take the American side in that fight, and Kit agreed. Better to be under China's thumb than caught in the crossfire between two superpowers.

Kit didn't really resent his American teammates, not individually anyway. They were intelligent and friendly fossil enthusiasts, just like himself. He just felt like a sherpa sometimes—the native guide useful for renting trucks and smoothing things over with the locals, but not anyone to be taken seriously. He knew that wasn't what they thought of him, or why Samira had hired him, but he struggled with the feeling just the same.

His "American" teammates weren't even Americans, not really. Gabby was from Argentina, a country whose rich Mesozoic geology had produced some of the world's best paleontologists. Arun had grown up in Bangladesh before going to college in New York City. Beth was the only one born in the US, and she had spent her childhood in Ethiopia, the daughter of missionaries. Samira, in a story Kit had never heard in full, was Beth's sister, an Ethiopian adopted by Beth's parents and raised as part of their family. They'd only moved back to Colorado as teenagers, when Samira started college.

Despite all that, the expedition itself was American, because America was where the money came from. Beth and Samira and Arun and Gabby all worked for American universities and paid for the trip and supplies with a grant from the

US government. He hoped someday his government would be able to afford grants like that.

A cloud of dust to the south warned of a visitor.

"We've got company," Samira said.

Some of the villagers in nearby Khai Nun owned vehicles —mostly aging and battered pickup trucks—but none as smooth and powerful as this one sounded. The dust gradually resolved into a black Toyota Landcruiser, apparently brand new. No local farmer could afford a car like that.

Samira stood, shielding her eyes from the sun, and walked out to meet the vehicle. The rest of them dropped their tools and gathered around her.

The passenger door opened, and a man stepped out. He was about fifty, wearing a tight-fitting khaki uniform with a rank and insignia on the breast pocket. It looked military, but Kit recognized it as the uniform most government officials wore. Professional titles and ranks were important in Thai culture, and many jobs had uniforms proclaiming the status of the wearer. This man was a police lieutenant, a man of substantial rank and influence in the district. Kit wondered if Samira knew that.

"We were told we have a week to shut down our operation," Samira said by way of greeting.

Kit winced. It was a confrontational beginning, very American, but bordering on rude in this culture.

"Miss Shannon?" the man asked in clear, barely-accented English.

"Doctor," Samira said.

"I beg your pardon?"

"Dr. Shannon, not Miss Shannon."

A beat of silence. "My apologies. I am Lieutenant Damrongsit Somjai of the Crime Suppression Division. I am not here about the deportation."

The lieutenant's eyes drifted past her. He would assume that, as a woman, she would not be truly in charge of the expedition, even if she held the title. Gender equality had made some modest inroads in Thailand—the ratio of female PhDs, for instance, was above average compared to other Asian countries. But many court proceedings were only valid with male witnesses, and women, even those with education and high position, were expected to defer to men.

Kit knew that Samira's skin color, too, would lessen her in the lieutenant's eyes. African slaves had never come to Thailand, but there was still racism here, much of it picked up from Western films and influence. Thais equated black skin with outdoor labor and little education, and advertisements throughout the country proclaimed the value of skin-whiteners to enhance beauty.

The lieutenant's gaze flicked past Beth and Gabby, hesitated briefly on Arun, and then settled, as Kit had known they would, on Kit himself. "Dr. Kittipoom Chongsuttanamanee?"

Kit pressed his palms together and bowed. "*Sawatdi khrap.*" He didn't approve of the man's prejudices, but he wouldn't confront him. That's not how things were done in Thailand. Besides, it was good to hear a fellow Thai pronounce his full name properly. Americans could never handle Thai names, and in Kit's years as an undergraduate at the University of Pennsylvania, few ever tried. He sometimes overheard them giggling about first names like "Dang" and "Siriporn," and the long last names they could never remember or pronounce.

The lieutenant returned his bow and spoke in Thai. "You must come with me please."

Kit felt his heart rate increase. Being taken away by the police couldn't be good.

Samira took a step forward so that she stood between the lieutenant and Kit. "Why?" she said in English. "What's the problem?"

The lieutenant spread open his arms. "I have no police officers here. I am not arresting this man. I need his help." He looked at Kit again. "We are investigating a fossil smuggling operation. I need you to look at a few things and tell me what you can."

"You found a fossil?" Gabby asked.

The lieutenant swiveled to look at her. "You are Gabriela Benitez?"

"It creeps me out that you know all our names," Beth said. She had the build of a girl, barely five feet tall and probably not much more than a hundred pounds, but she could radiate ferocity when she wanted to. "There's something weird going on here."

"Agreed," Samira said. "And we're not going to let you just take him away. If Kit goes, I go too."

Kit didn't think he needed a babysitter, but he felt a rush of affection for her for standing up for him.

The lieutenant took a step back and gave another slight bow. "As you wish. Now please..." He indicated the car.

Kit followed the lieutenant to the car and climbed into the back. Samira joined him, folding her long legs into the narrow space. A driver sat behind the wheel. Lieutenant Somjai took the front passenger seat.

The driver turned the car around, kicking up another cloud of dust, and gunned it down the road away from the site. The dirt path eventually led to a paved road, straight and flat for miles, studded with tin-roofed houses and rough-hewn market stands made from wooden stakes and shaded with grass thatching. They passed Huai Lak, the lake that provided water for many of the surrounding villages. Beyond the lake, green scrub and brown fields stretched in every direction. A pair of pickup trucks passed them, loaded ten feet high with brown sugar cane.

"Can you tell us what this is about?" Kit asked.

"I'm sorry, I do not wish many people to know," Somjai said. "A man has been killed. Someone from Khai Nun."

Kit traded a look with Samira. Khai Nun was the village where the team had been staying. "Who?"

"A man named Nikorn Paknikorn. He was found...well, you will see."

Nikorn. The man was a farmer, like most of the villagers, with a young and pretty wife he doted on.

The car turned off the paved road, and they bounced across an open field toward the mountains. Kit saw flashing lights in the distance, and soon they pulled up to a small circle of police cars and yellow tape. There was nothing here—no buildings, no crops—just rocky ground and brush.

He and Samira climbed out and made their way with Somjai to the center of the gathering. A man lay on the ground, his shirt dark with blood, his chest a wreck of torn flesh. Kit had never seen a murder victim before. He covered his mouth, afraid he might be sick, but he couldn't look away. Did a knife do that kind of damage? A bullet? He didn't know.

"It is this we want you to see," Somjai said. He indicated an uneven block of stone, roughly hewn, lying on the ground.

What Kit saw there set his heart racing even more than the corpse. A clearly-defined skull, vertebrae, and wings stood out in sharp relief in the stone, the texture of its feathers easily visible. It was a maniraptoran, probably a dromaeosaurid, and at first glance, it appeared to be the same species as the three specimens their team had been slowly teasing out of the mountainside for months. It had the same fan-like tail, and most tellingly, two opposable thumbs on each hand. This one's skull, however, was in place and intact, which would provide much more data on how these creatures lived and what they ate.

Kit felt his anger rise. Well-preserved, yes, but pieces had been snapped off and the whole exposed structure scraped and chipped. This wasn't erosion, but damage caused recently by incompetent removal. Worse, it had been torn out of its environment without study. Paleontologists solved the mysteries of fossils in two ways: by studying the bones themselves, and by studying the surrounding rock layers. Understanding the rock strata around a find involved weeks of painstaking geological survey. Trying to answer questions about a fossil without knowing where it came from was like asking a detective to solve a crime with no access to the crime scene.

He glanced back at the dead body, partially blocked from view by the detectives leaning over it. As far as he was concerned, if Nikorn was the smuggler who did this, the man deserved everything he got.

"So what's the story?" he asked. "How did he die?"

Somjai stood with a careful stretch, as if his leg muscles hurt. "We were hoping you might help us determine that. Is this fossil very valuable?"

"It's priceless."

Somjai smiled as if those muscles hurt, too. "In terms of money, though. Could it be sold for a lot?"

"I guess so. Something this complete with those features—the feathers I mean—would make it a top end collectors item. I'm also interested in what looks like substantial pneumatization of the skull—"

"How much?" Somjai said.

"Pneumatization? Quite a bit. See these large depressions in the jaw? Those are cavities similar to our sinuses. The relative size indicates that this species had quite a remarkable sense of smell—"

"Not that. How much money?"

Kit sighed. "Would it sell for? I don't know. We're not in the business of selling fossils."

"Maybe a couple hundred thousand," Samira said.

"Dollars?" Somjai whistled. "That kind of money would go a long way out here."

"Goes a long way anywhere," Kit said. "Doesn't look like it was worth the risk for this man, though. What happened? Was he killed by a competitor?"

The lieutenant grimaced. "If he was, then why leave the fossil behind? If you kill somebody for money, you don't leave the money lying on the ground."

"Maybe the murderer didn't know how valuable it was," Samira suggested. "Or maybe he couldn't lift it by himself and planned to come back with help."

Something caught Kit's eye and he leaned in to examine it more closely. "Look at this," he said, pointing. On the uneven surface of one of the broken pieces, at the center of the bone, there was a tiny dark speck. "Is that what I think it is?"

Samira peered at it. "It could be," she said, a spark of excitement in her voice. "We'd have to dissolve it down in some weak acid to be sure, see if anything is left."

"It could be what?" Somjai asked.

"Soft tissue," Samira said. "Fragments of blood vessels, trapped inside the bones and preserved by the iron in its blood."

"Is that rare?"

"Very," Kit said. "There have been, what, a dozen cases of red blood cells or proteins extracted from dinosaur bones?"

"This is blood?" Somjai asked. He seemed excited. "Like with DNA?"

Samira laughed. "No, no, nothing like that. The DNA breaks down. We're talking millions of years here."

Somjai pointed. "It's a velociraptor, yes? Like in the American movies?"

Kit shook his head politely. He wasn't surprised. Most people's understanding of dinosaurs came from what they saw in *Jurassic Park* and its endless sequels—American misinformation that was exported worldwide. He was used to using it as a comparison point for explanations.

"The raptors in the movies were dromaeosaurids," he said. "They called them velociraptors, but they were closer in size to *Deinonychus*. *Velociraptor* was a lot smaller, and both were feathered like birds, not green and scaly. This isn't a dromaeosaurid, though. The snout is much too long, the legs too slender, and the number of teeth makes me think it's a troodontid. If so, it's the largest troodontid ever found— they're rarely larger than a chicken."

"If the DNA were preserved in the right way, though," Somjai said stubbornly. "Like in amber? Then it could be retrieved?"

"You don't understand," Samira said. "If it's thousands of years, then yes, in rare instances, like if the bodies are dessicated or frozen in permafrost, we might retrieve a fragment of damaged DNA. But sixty-six million years? That's more than a thousand times older than the oldest DNA ever retrieved. Sorry. It's not possible."

The lieutenant's expression soured. "Thank you for your help. I'll drive you back."

"Wait," Samira said. "What about the fossil?"

"It is evidence."

"It needs to be preserved. Wrapped and moved properly, so it isn't damaged. If there is any soft tissue there, the proteins won't last long in the open air."

"It's not yours, Dr. Shannon. It's the property of Thailand."

"We're not trying to take it off of you," Kit said. *Much as I'd like to*, he didn't add. "We just want to make sure there are professionals looking after it. The university should be involved. I'm a professor there; please, let me help you. We both want this evidence kept safe."

"If you let us study it, we might be able to answer some questions for you. Figure out where it came from, for instance," Samira said. Kit shot her a sideways glance. It was very unlikely they would be able to pinpoint where in the miles of surrounding mountains this fossil came from just by examining it. That was why it was so important to thoroughly study a fossil's surroundings before pulling it out. But Kit didn't contradict her.

Somjai, however, seemed suspicious. "This would be worth a lot to you as well, yes? Not in money, perhaps, but in prestige and published papers and the respect of your colleagues."

"Of course. But I'm not suggesting—"

"You would certainly appreciate its value more than any of the poor farmers who live in this region. But maybe you have no permission to dig in that place."

"What place?" Samira asked.

Somjai shrugged. "The place it came from."

"He's suggesting that you took it," Kit said.

Samira's expressive face turned insolent. "We're *scientists,*" she said. "We don't steal and destroy valuable fossils."

"Perhaps," Somjai said. "But then perhaps you are very angry when someone else does steal them."

"Look, there's no question we consider this fossil valuable," Samira said. "And yeah, smuggling makes us angry. But if it had been us, we would have treated it with more care. And we wouldn't have left it lying here on the ground."

Somjai shrugged again. "Maybe you can't lift it and plan to come back later with help."

"Please," Kit said. "We're on the same side. We both want to know what happened."

Somjai met his gaze. "I will let *you* come into our lab and examine, Dr. Chongsuttanamanee. No one else." He gave Samira an unpleasant smile. "Besides, you are leaving the country soon, yes?"

CHAPTER FOUR

S amira woke in the village the next morning to the sound of the *puyaiban*, Headman Kaew, making his morning announcements. He spoke in Isan, the main dialect of the northeastern Lao language, his words booming loudly over the crackle and squeal of the antiquated speaker system he kept on his roof. She understood only snatches, but it didn't matter. Most of it concerned local affairs, such as whose cow had successfully given birth the night before, or who in the village had received a letter and should come to pick it up.

Samira yawned and opened her eyes. The olive green fabric of her tent glowed with diffuse morning light. For a brief moment, it felt like every other morning, waking up in Khai Nun at sunrise to begin another day of excavation. Then she remembered: Today was their last day. After six months of preparation and two months of work, they would be thrown out of the country with no idea when they might return.

She threw back the flap of her sleeping bag and sat up. Cope and Marsh squawked and marched back and forth, clamoring to be fed. It was always a race to see who would wake her first, Headman Kaew or the crows. She stroked

Cope's head with a finger, and Marsh butted his head in the way to get a turn.

Cope and Marsh were maniraptors too, of course, just like the creatures whose bones the team had unearthed. Modern birds were descendents of coelurosaurian dinosaurs and shared many of the same traits: breastbones, three-fingered hands, curved wrists, specialized lungs, hollow bones, and feathers. Once you knew what to look for, it was easy to see the inner velociraptor hiding behind their beady eyes.

After throwing on a reasonably clean pair of shorts and a T-shirt, she stepped outside. She grabbed the traditional tao stove, a conical metal bucket with a clay insert that cooked food with remarkably little fuel, and hurled a few pieces of charcoal into it. She jammed it into the earth, feeling angry and helpless. She threw chicken pieces into a wok with some oil and jabbed at them until they sizzled and spat. The warm stove provided some relief from the early morning chill. By noon, the sun's heat would turn the dry plateau into a furnace, but this early in the day she could still see her breath condensing in white puffs of fog.

"Wow, a hot breakfast," Beth said, ducking out of her tent. "Sami, you didn't have to."

Samira shrugged. "Last morning here. Might as well make the most of it."

"I can't believe we're leaving after what we just found."

"We're not *leaving*, we're being deported," Samira said. "It's criminal."

Beth crouched by the stove and warmed her hands. "We have a lot to keep us busy for a while. And they'll have to let us back in eventually."

Samira tried an answering smile, but she wasn't sure it came out right.

They camped in the field in back of Headman Kaew's house. It limited the manioc he could plant there this year, but they paid him well for the use of the land, probably more than he could get for the manioc, and for a good deal less effort. Kaew's wife, Yai, came out of the house, smiling all the way, with a bowl full of fingerroot, chilis, and Isan sausage to add to the wok. Beth and Samira both pressed their palms together and bowed, thanking her. When Samira had first come to Thailand, the *wai* gesture felt silly, but now it came as easily as breathing. If someone had offered to shake her hand, she might not have remembered quite how to do it.

Everyone in the village had been overwhelmingly friendly to their team. She would miss the gentle kindness and generosity of these people, who knew little and cared less about paleontology, but worked the land with diligence and cared for their families and community the way they had for generations. And, apparently, occasionally smuggled fossils and murdered each other. She supposed no place on Earth was perfect.

She left the stove and made her way along the well-beaten path to the outhouse. Most village homes had electricity and running water—when they worked—but indoor plumbing had not yet come to Khai Nun. The outhouse belonged to Headman Kaew's home, which was traditional rural Thai in construction, with the living area on the second floor and the first floor reserved for livestock. All of it—even the outhouse —took on the too-bright intensity of a location long familiar that she might now never see again. She was going to miss this place.

When she returned to the camp, she helped Beth distribute the chicken stir fry onto tin plates. Arun's tent fluttered open and Gabby came out of it, followed by Arun, holding her hand. Samira raised an eyebrow. She hadn't seen a relationship between the two of them coming, but then, that wasn't surprising. She'd never been very good at reading people. She wondered if it had been going on for a while, or if the melancholy of their last night here had brought them together.

Arun collapsed to the ground like a marionnette with its strings cut. He groaned and pressed fingers into his eyelids. "Why does it have to be morning?"

Gabby laughed and stroked his hair. "Someone dipped too deeply into the *lao khao* last night."

"It was a party," Arun complained. "We're leaving. I couldn't exactly refuse."

"Fanfan's *lao khao* is best used for stripping paint," Gabby said. "I'm surprised you survived." *Lao khao* was a local moonshine that, like the chicken, bananas, limes, lemongrass, and vegetables that made up most of their meals, came directly from this village.

Arun massaged his temples. "I'm not sure I did. It packs a vicious kick, that's for sure."

Samira was tired, too, having driven the truck on a three hour round trip to the Kalasin airstrip the night before. She had contracted with a pilot to fly their fossils and rock samples to Bangkok, where they would be packed into the shipping container they had rented. The container would in turn be loaded onto a giant freighter with thousands of identical containers for the long trek across the ocean to San Francisco, where—if all went well—it would be loaded onto a tractor-trailer and hauled cross-country to the University of Colorado.

The cargo consisted of three crates packed with straw. Inside, wrapped in hardened casts of plaster-soaked toilet paper, sat their fossil maniraptors. She had paid the pilot and watched him and his crew load it onto his plane. She'd dealt with the man before and trusted his reputation, but it still terrified her to leave her precious fossils with someone to whom they meant nothing more than a paycheck. Like leaving one's children with a teenage babysitter, she imagined. Reasonable and sometimes necessary, but still nerve-wracking.

Yawning, Samira picked up a pot of brown rice that she had set aside with some of the chicken and carried it back toward the village square. The crows followed, cawing insistently. She circled Headman Kaew's house just as the monks arrived in a procession of orange robes and shaved heads. Joining the other villagers gathered around them, she scooped some food into each monk's alms bowl. The gifts would be all that the monks had to eat that day. The monks blessed her in return, balancing her karma.

Samira didn't really believe in karma, or making merit, or any of that. But last day or not, while her team rented space in this little village, she would honor her neighbors' customs and treat their culture with respect.

A novice monk trailed at the back of the procession. He was a boy, no more than seven, his head still raw from the shaving razor. Most boys in Thailand became monks at some point, usually only for a few weeks, and most men did at some stage of life as well. The boy stared at her as he passed. Not many black women traveled through the rural villages of the Khorat Plateau, and Samira's height made her stand out in the crowd. Marsh chose that moment to squawk loudly, and the boy jumped a foot in the air.

The other monks laughed at him, and a few pointed at her and said, "Manohara!" She placed a large piece of chicken in the boy's bowl and smiled at him. The crows eyed the chicken jealously. "Hush, you'll get some, too," she scolded.

The roar of an engine caught her attention. She turned to see three identical black SUVs kicking up dust as they came into view along the road into the village. The villagers stepped back to make room. Gabby, Arun, and Beth quickly joined them, watching the oncoming vehicles with a worried expression at the oncoming vehicles.

"What's happening?" Arun asked.

"I don't know. Lieutenant Somjai again?" The lieutenant had dropped Samira back at the site the day before, but Kit had stayed with the smuggled fossil, and they hadn't seen him since.

Six Thai men in military uniforms—true Army uniforms this time, not police—stepped out of the cars.

The man in front scanned the crowd and settled on her. "Samira Shannon?"

"Doctor," she corrected automatically.

"You and your team are to come with us for questioning and immediate deportment."

"There's no need for that," Samira said. "We're leaving, just like we were told. We head to Bangkok tonight, and our flight leaves tomorrow morning."

"I'm afraid that is unacceptable," the man said. "We are detaining you as a suspected American spy and CIA operative, illegally violating the sovereignty of Thailand."

Samira's mouth dropped open. "What?"

"We're here legally under a research visa," Beth said calmly. "We can show you our papers."

Samira knew the best way to deal with Thai bureaucracy was with patient reason, but after everything that had happened this week, she didn't have much patience left. "This is nonsense," she said. "It's not enough to throw us out, you have to harass us, too? I'm a *scientist*. I'm not a spy. It's ridiculous. We're up here in the ass end of nowhere—just what do you think I'm spying on? The rice paddies? I've never *met* anybody from the CIA, never mind—"

"Sami," Beth said.

"What?" Samira snapped. When Beth didn't answer, she looked at her for a long beat. "Oh, you've got to be kidding me."

"They contributed to the research grant," Beth said.

"The *CIA*?"

"I don't know why—I wouldn't think paleontology was generally their thing—but we needed the money. I wasn't going to say no. And it's not like it was a secret. Well, it was sort of a secret; they used some kind of corporate cover. But it's not like it was classified or anything." Beth turned to the soldiers. "I'm sure we can clear this up quickly. We don't work for the CIA. We don't know or care about your politics. We're not spies, and as my sister points out, there's nothing around here to spy on anyway."

"You will come with us now," the soldier said. "All of you. You will leave this country only after all our questions have been answered. And once you leave, you will never return."

There was nothing to do but obey. Cope and Marsh squawked forlornly and flapped in the dust as the car drove away.

SAMIRA HAD NEVER BEEN in a holding cell before, but she didn't think most of them came with child-sized desks and a chalkboard. The desks were piled in one corner of the otherwise empty cinderblock room. The single window was blocked with thick metal bars. Apparently this was a repurposed elementary school. It didn't make the lock on the door any less effective.

The chalkboard was scrawled with messages in Thai script drawn with fingers in chalk dust. Samira couldn't read it, but she guessed the words were obscenities. Four Thai men lounged in the room already, one asleep on the floor, the other three sitting against the wall. The arrival of their team provoked barely a flicker of interest. Samira wondered how long the men had been here, and for what crimes.

Samira sat in the corner farthest from them, and Arun and Beth joined her against the wall. Gabby sighed and collapsed into a sitting position, facing the three of them. "The CIA?" she asked Beth. "Really?"

"They went through open channels," Beth said. "A guy showed up at the lab, offered a grant, and I took it. There were no strings attached, no requests to spy for them or do anything shady. Just some much-appreciated funds. I figured, the CIA is a big organization, they do lots of things. They've got that factbook, right? They compile information about places and cultures all over the world. Maybe they'll ask us questions when we get back about what things are like in rural Thailand." She attempted a smile. "Feels pretty naive now."

"There's got to be more to it," Samira said. "Why is the Thai military bothering with us at all? Why do they care? There are lots of Americans here, most of them in Bangkok or Chiang Mai or one of the beach resorts. We're nothing special."

"You think maybe there *is* some secret facility out here? Something they don't want the CIA to know about?" Beth asked.

"Must be where they keep the alien technology," Arun said.

Beth looked at Samira. "What about the murdered man you and Kit saw? Could it be connected to that?"

Samira shrugged. "Doesn't seem likely. He was just a poor farmer smuggling fossils for the money. Probably shot by his accomplice. I don't see how that would warrant attention from the military."

Arun scratched his face. "You remember that guy in Bangkok?"

"What guy?" Samira asked.

"When we first got here, that day you spent all afternoon at the visa office. We took water taxis up and down the Chao Phraya, visiting the temples. Every time we turned around, there was this same guy, watching us. We thought we were being set up for some kind of theft or scam or something. You think he was an intelligence officer?"

"I don't know. None of this smells right," Samira said. "It's not just about our funding sources. There's something they don't want us to know, and they're afraid we're here to find it out."

"How do we convince them we're not?" Arun asked.

"Good question." Beth glanced at the men sitting on the other side of the room. She lowered her voice. "I think we should play nice. Thai people value respect and humility, and they have a lot of power to make things hard for us. If you shout at someone in authority here, he loses face, and then he feels like he has to punish you or he'll appear weak." Beth didn't look at Samira, but Samira could feel her pointed gaze all the same. "Speak calmly and politely—be obsequious, even. It's not like there's an embassy nearby to help us out. If they feel threatened, they could keep us here for a very long time."

"So don't act like Americans, in other words," Arun said.

"Remember, our fossils aren't out of the country yet. They could easily block our shipping container in Bangkok harbor."

"We have a contract allowing us to export those," Samira objected.

"A contract with a government that no longer exists," Beth said. "The new administration can choose not to honor it. They could say we're stealing their national treasures."

Arun rested his head in his hands. "I'm a little more worried they won't let *us* out of the country."

"True enough," Gabby said. "This morning I hated the thought that they were making us leave. Now I'm terrified they won't let us."

The lock rattled, and the door swung open. Two soldiers came in, one with a hand on his holstered gun. "Dr. Shannon?"

Beth and Samira answered at the same time. "Yes?"

The soldier pointed at Samira. "The colonel will see you now."

Samira traded a look with the others and stood. She knew that at some level she was scared, but it didn't feel that way. She felt angry. She reminded herself of Beth's advice and took a deep breath. *Play nice, Samira. Get us out of this.*

The men brought her to the end of a hallway and into a

room that could have been an athletic director's office, though it displayed no inspirational posters or team paraphernalia. A gaunt, bald man in glasses and a glaringly white uniform stood by the desk. The three stars on each shoulder and the ribbons and gold braid screamed high rank and importance. She pressed her palms together and bowed deeply. Rank was important around here, and fortunately the soldiers had told her his, since she didn't know how to interpret the insignia. "Colonel?"

He returned the *wai*, though curtly. "We know who you are and who you work for," he said.

A soldier indicated a wooden chair and she sat. "That has never been a secret," she said, trying to stay calm and show respect. "My name is Dr. Samira Shannon, and I work for the University of Colorado."

"You are CIA," the man insisted. "Do not pretend. We know already."

Samira took a deep breath. "Our project was funded in part by the CIA," she acknowledged. "I just found that out today. But I have never been their employee. If they want something from my research, I don't know what it is. Please." She opened her hands, palms up. "I'm exactly who I seem to be. No secrets."

The colonel stepped around the desk and tried to loom over her, though even sitting, she was nearly as tall. "Where are the rest of your finds?"

"The rest?" She thought of their fossils, the work of months, probably being loaded into a shipping container at that moment. "I don't know what you mean."

The colonel glanced briefly at the two soldiers who had brought her in. They stood on either side of her and placed a hand on each of her shoulders, pressing roughly. She started to breathe harder, really scared now.

She shook them off. "Don't touch me." They put their hands right back again.

"The man you killed, we found that one," the colonel said. "Where are the others?"

"We didn't kill anyone!"

He grabbed her hair and leaned his face in close enough that she could smell the oil on his skin. His men prevented her from pulling away. "The others!"

She didn't want to tell him—a man like this could stop their shipping container with a phone call—but she didn't have much choice. "I loaded them on a plane at Kalasin airfield last night," she said. "By now they're at Bangkok harbor."

He curled his lips and made a spitting noise. "You lie," he said. He stood and walked out of the room. The soldiers hauled her to her feet and dragged her after him.

"No, that's the truth!" she said. "I can show you the invoice and the customs forms. Everything is in order."

The colonel strode across the hall and stiff-armed his way through a set of double doors. Samira followed, pushed along by her captors.

They entered a larger, high-ceilinged room, like a small gymnasium, though the floor was carpeted concrete and there were no bleachers or basketball hoops. In the middle of the floor, surrounded by an explosion of straw, white plaster dust, and the remains of three wooden crates, sat her carefully sealed fossils, looking as though they had been torn open with a crowbar. They weren't in Bangkok after all. Clearly, they had never made it off the ground.

Samira lost it. "What is this?" she shouted. With a violent twist of her shoulders, she threw off the soldiers' grips and ran to the demolished crates. The ancient remains, preserved for millions of years, were now scored by metal tools or broken into pieces. Splinters of fossilized bone littered the floor. She whirled on the colonel, advancing. "Who gave you the right? What did you think, we were smuggling drugs or something? We could have *showed* you. You could have *X-rayed* them, not torn them to pieces like drunken barbarians." She was far beyond politeness now, but she couldn't help herself. These irreplaceable artifacts had been destroyed by thugs who couldn't tell the difference between spies and paleontologists. "You bastards are nothing more than criminals; I don't care what uniforms you wear. This is theft. It's destruction of United States property. We have a contract for these fossils, and I'm going to make sure you—"

"Ms. Shannon." The colonel's sharp bark cut through her tirade as his goons grabbed her arms from both sides.

"Doctor!" she shouted in his face. She didn't care anymore. They couldn't do anything worse than what they'd already done.

"We know about these already, of course," he said. "We followed you on your midnight drive and intercepted them. It is the *others* we want. Those dug from the hills at Na Khu and Lup Lao and Phu Pha Yol. If not for the murdered villager, you might have slipped away, but now we know. You can not hope to play the innocent. We know. How do you say it? The game is up."

Samira stared at him, her rage turning to disbelief. The *others*? The other what? Fossils? *More* fossils like the one Lieutenant Somjai had showed them, dug up from sites all over the province?

"Smugglers," she said. "Can't you tell the difference? We have nothing to do with that. We don't know anything about it."

"If you don't tell me the truth," the colonel said in a quiet, conversational tone, "you will never leave this place, and your family will never know what happened to you."

That stopped her. She took a long, deep breath, remembering Beth's advice. "Sir," she said, swallowing bile. "Respected colonel. Please listen to me. We are scientists. We care, most of all, that fossils are removed carefully and that discoveries are published to the world. We don't smuggle, we don't operate in secret, and we don't"—she bit back the rage that surged into her throat at the thought of the demolished artifacts behind her—"*destroy* things. The fossil found with the dead man was dug out hastily and unprofessionally, with complete disregard for science. It. Wasn't. Us."

As she spoke, her mind raced. Who was this man? He wasn't a policeman or a customs official. He was a high-ranking soldier or intelligence agent. So what did he care about fossils? He thought the CIA was involved—why would the CIA smuggle fossils out of Thailand? It made no sense. Were the fossils a cover for some other secret export? Possibly, but it seemed unlikely. There had to be easier, less conspicuous ways to get goods or information out of the country.

The soldiers forced her back across the hall to the tiny office. There the colonel peppered her with questions about every detail of their schedule and finances, about her university, her investors, even her parents and her childhood. She answered them all as simply and honestly as she could. As her anger cooled, it was replaced once again by fear. If they thought she was a spy, to what lengths might they go to extract information? The new regime wanted to show they were tough on American infiltration. As the colonel had implied, they could bury the four of them in a secret prison cellar somewhere and never let them out. With China's support, they wouldn't have to cave to American pressure.

Finally, after what seemed like hours, they dragged her back to the classroom holding cell. The others were where she had left them, though they looked considerably more harried and anxious than before. They stood as she entered, desperate for news.

"Are you okay?"

"What happened?"

"What do they want?"

Samira shook her head, exhausted and demoralized. "They think we're spies."

"That's crazy," Beth said. "What's going to happen to us?"

"I don't know. But I think we're in big trouble." She started to tell them about the demolished fossils, but before she could, one of the soldiers took Beth's arm. "Bethany Shannon," he said. "You will come with us."

CHAPTER FIVE

K it's back hurt and his arms ached. Ever since Lieutenant Somjai had given him permission, he'd been hard at work, painstakingly scraping and sanding at the smuggled fossil to reveal its secrets. They had denied his request to transport the fossil to Sirindhorn Museum, a geology museum in Kalasin province and the only place in the country with fossil exhibits and research facilities. It was only an hour's drive away, but Somjai had been utterly unwilling to listen to reason.

In fact, Somjai did not seem to be the one in charge. A surprising number of men in Royal Thai Army uniforms had joined them, and although Somjai was a police lieutenant, not military at all, he seemed to defer to the soldiers. Instead of Sirindhorn, they trucked the fossils in the other direction to what seemed like a defunct school, a collection of ugly concrete buildings surrounding a central grassy area gone to weeds. The grassy area featured a rusty metal slide and a swing set with only one remaining swing hanging limply by a single chain.

The Army had taken over the facility. The road onto the

grounds was blocked with debris and manned by soldiers with carbines. A dozen Jeeps and five canvas-draped trucks stood in rows by the main entrance, and more security guarded the doors. Three black SUVs sat parked further down by one of the other buildings.

What was going on? He'd thought of this a straightforward murder and smuggling investigation. Why was the Army involved? The dead man was a poor farmer. No one of importance, at least not to anyone outside his village. It didn't make sense.

The soldiers hauled the smuggled fossil into the building while Kit hovered nervously, terrified they would drop it. They brought it to a room that must once have been a chemistry classroom, with thick black countertops and sinks at regular intervals, and set it carefully on the wider table at the front.

"You can work here," Somjai said. "Do you need anything else?"

Kit gave an astonished laugh. "Anything *else?*" There was nothing here but bare countertops.

"Well, what do you need, then?"

"I need a lab! A real lab like at Sirindhorn, as I've been telling you."

"Out of the question," Somjai said. "Tell me what equipment you need, and I'll see what I can do."

Kit rolled his eyes. "Let's see. I need a stereo dissecting microscope, with a wide focal range and multiple lenses. I need it mounted on an articulated boom arm, so I can shift it anywhere on the specimen I need to examine." He counted off on his fingers. "I need fiberoptic branch lights and a range of fine steel needles of different diameters and shaped points, along with a pin vise to hold the smaller ones. I'll need to sharpen them regularly, which means a bench grinder with a diamond wheel. Oh, and I'll need an air compressor with hoses and a pressure regulator to blow away particulates. And

I don't suppose you have any airscribes in the closet, do you? Those are handheld tools with vibrating carbide needles, manufactured specifically for fossil preparation. Standard kit for an Army camp, I'm sure."

Somjai held up his hand. "Enough. You asked to come here, so set your sarcasm aside. You're right, I know nothing about paleontology. But when the Army wants to accomplish something, they can bring enormous resources to bear. Make your list, and I'll see what I can do."

Chagrined, Kit made a quick *wai* of apology. "If you have any kind of small steel tools, awls or screwdrivers, for instance, and some sandpaper, I could make a start. Some glue would be nice, too. Any kind of real progress, though, will take real equipment."

Somjai nodded sharply. "Make your list."

Soldiers returned almost immediately with several tool-boxes. Normally, Kit wouldn't dare to prepare a fossil with such crude tools, but this specimen had been excavated so unprofessionally that large amounts of the surrounding stone remained attached. Cruder tools could be used to remove much of the excess without striking too close to the bone.

He had little hope that the Army would find adequate equipment unless they confiscated it from Sirindhorn Museum itself. But whatever security precautions prevented them from allowing him to work there surely also prevented them from raiding a high profile scientific lab. And there *weren't* any other labs with that kind of equipment, not in this province anyway, and probably not in all of Northern Thailand.

Still, as the Buddha said, happiness comes to those who appreciate what they have. Kit picked out an awl and a scrap of sandpaper and got to work.

FIVE HOURS LATER, exhausted and hungry, Kit stood surrounded by rock shards and dust. He had dislodged many of the larger pieces of stone, but without finer tools, he couldn't address the fossil itself. Which meant that despite his efforts, he knew no more about the creature than when he'd started.

He brushed off his clothing and opened the door of the classroom, intending to ask a soldier where he could get something to eat. To his surprise, Lieutenant Somjai stood in front of the door, his fist raised to knock. Behind him, two soldiers lugged a large box full of equipment.

"Dr. Chongsuttanamanee," Somjai said. "How are you progressing?"

"Slowly," Kit said.

"Would more hands speed the work?"

"Absolutely not," Kit said, aghast at the thought of clumsy soldiers bashing away at his delicate specimen.

"Just a suggestion," Somjai said. "We brought some things for you."

The soldiers hauled in three large boxes, one at a time. Astonished, Kit started removing the contents. They were dentist's tools. An array of steel picks of various shapes and sizes. An air compressor with hoses and fine nozzles to direct the flow. A variety of handheld rotary tools with both grinding and needle-shaped tips. Vises and support apparatus. Driers and suction tubes. And in the last box, a quality microscope and the pieces of a metal arm Kit recognized as one used to move an overhead light into position.

"Not sure if that boom will hold the microscope as it is," Somjai said. "We might need to shore it up some."

"This is brilliant," Kit said, amazed. It still fell short of equipment that was designed for the purpose—the needle tips weren't really fine enough for the most delicate work, and lateral vibration tended to work better than rotary motion to free matrix from the bone—but given the situation, it was far better than he'd thought possible.

It had never occurred to him how similar dentist's tools were to those of a paleontology lab. He wondered if it had been Somjai or some bright field quartermaster who'd had the idea. He also wondered what poor dentist had just had all his equipment confiscated by the Army, and if they had compensated him for it. But that wasn't his problem.

The equipment made it possible for him to do real investigation, perhaps answer some questions about what sort of creature this had been when it was alive. He forgot all about eating and got to work.

He started with the skull. Normally this might not have been the best idea, since the skull was generally the most difficult and tricky portion of a skeleton to explore. However, it was also the most likely to yield significant findings. Given the tenuous nature of his situation, Kit decided he needed to discover what he could as quickly as possible, in case the Army got tired of him and decided to throw him out.

Unlike the specimens Samira's team had excavated, which were probably en route to the United States by now, this one featured an intact skull. The skeleton seemed more damaged by erosion and the incompetent method of its removal than by the pressures of fossilization, and the skull was no exception. It had retained much of its original shape. The skull was large for its body size, roughly the volume of a human skull, though arranged much differently. The jaw protruded from the head and contained serrated, blade-like teeth, indicating a primarily carnivorous diet.

It shared many skull features with troodontids, long considered among the most intelligent dinosaurs because of their proportionately larger brain cavity. But another feature caught Kit's attention. The skull showed evidence of huge olfactory bulbs, the neural structures involved in the sense of smell.

The bulbs themselves were soft tissue, of course, and thus long since destroyed, but he could see the space in the cranial vault where they would have been. Large olfactory bulbs correlated with a strong sense of smell, both in terms of sensitivity and the ability to distinguish among a large variety of chemicals. Tyrannosaurs, for instance, were known to have had an excellent sense of smell by their large olfactory bulbs.

The cavities in front of him dwarfed those found in *T. rex*. An olfactory bulb inspection usually required a CT scan or at least an endocast, but Kit could *see* the cavities unaided if he peered inside at the right angle. They were enormous, far larger than those of any animal he'd ever heard of, living or dead. Which meant either that the cavities that usually housed olfactory bulbs contained organs with some other purpose—what, he couldn't imagine—or that this creature had been able to detect smells farther away and more accurately than any animal that had ever walked the Earth.

Kit rested the point of a curved steel pick on a thin layer of rock adhering to the bone. He switched on a rotary tool meant to clean teeth and rested it against the handle of the pick. The rotary tool caused the pick to vibrate gently, which after a few seconds caused the stone to crumble and fall away from the bone without damaging the bone's fine features.

He worked his way down toward the rock that encased the creature's body. As he did so, he noticed a fissure that was stained with some kind of greenish residue. He touched it gingerly. It was dry, but soft and raised, clearly not something that had been there when the rock was chiseled out of the surrounding hillside. It looked almost as if it had bubbled *out* of the rock.

With a straight pick, he started to pry at the fissure, using a small hammer to tap lightly on the pick and dislodge small shards. After several attempts, he felt the pick give and slide inside. Afraid he might have damaged the fossil, he drew back, and a thin green liquid bubbled out from where he had pierced it.

Kit leaned in, astonished. What was it? Sixty-six million year old swamp water? But still liquid? That was impossible. Then the smell reached him. Sickly sweet and decaying, with a hint of petroleum. It reached up his sinuses and took hold, filling him with a sudden and uncontrollable terror. This smell meant danger in a way his animal brain seemed to comprehend at once, before his conscious mind had time to process the sensation. It meant menace and pursuit and rending teeth and fire and imminent death.

He stumbled backward, gasping for breath, his body telling him to flee. He tripped over an empty box and landed hard on his backside. Above him loomed a giant brown bird. But no, not a bird. Its plumage, talons, and furtive movements were birdlike, but its arms ended in hands and claws, and its long jaw bristled with needle-sharp teeth. Its body was covered with protofeathers, the filament-like precursors to the feathers of modern birds. He knew it was the maniraptor, even as his brain shouted that this was impossible. It darted its head forward as if it might attack. Kit shrieked and scrambled backward.

It had to be some kind of hallucinogen. The creature wasn't actually there; something had caused his brain to transform the long-dead fossil on the table into the illusion of a living, breathing dinosaur. Still, the overwhelming sense of terror kept him crawling backward until he hit the wall. He cried out, certain to his bones that he was about to be torn limb from limb. It was the reflex of quarry cornered by a predator. He looked up from the floor into its cold yellow eyes and knew he would die.

Abruptly, the vision changed. He was outside, high on a bare hill at night, still looking up. The chemistry classroom was gone. A vast array of stars blanketed the open sky. Kit had learned the constellations as a boy, but he saw none of the familiar shapes. Around him on the hill, in every direction, stood more of the brown feathered maniraptors, all of them gazing up at the sky. Hundreds of them, standing motionless. They seemed to be arranged in some kind of pattern, each standing an equal distance away from those closest, as if preparing for a dance. Kit realized with a start that *he* was one of the maniraptors, with his own place on the hill among the others.

The vision vanished. He sat shaking on the floor of the classroom, the dinosaurs and the hillside and the sky all gone.

He tried to get a grip on himself. *Think rationally.*

What could have caused such a thing? The most straight-forward answer was that whatever chemical had been trapped in the rock fissure had a powerful hallucinogenic effect, and his brain had concocted the things that he saw. Nothing more than a drug-induced dream. The power and vividness of the vision made him want to question that hypothesis, but he knew such experiences could feel quite real. Perhaps some kind of fungus had wormed its way into a crack in the rock, and had fermented over time to produce a potent cocktail.

He thought of the murdered smuggler and the fossil apparently abandoned in haste. Could this hallucinogen have been what they were after? Regardless, he had to report to the lieutenant what he had discovered.

WHEN SOMJAI CAME BACK into the room, he was accom-panied by six other men. Three wore uniforms of the Royal Thai Army, like most of the men he'd seen at the complex. The other three wore uniforms he didn't recognize, a brilliant white instead of olive, with epaulets and badges of rank. Somjai introduced them as members of the Weapons Research division. "The colonel will join us shortly," Somjai said.

They stood in the small classroom, not speaking, for five minutes that seemed like an hour. Finally, the door opened to admit an older, bespectacled man who, despite a bald head and a face wrinkled with age, held himself rigidly erect and wore a proud frown. His white uniform shirt was perfectly pressed and practically glowed. The other men saluted him sharply, using the new Thai military salute invented by King Vajiralongkorn.

Kit pressed his hands together and bowed low. "Respected colonel," he said.

The colonel's expression didn't change, but his gaze impaled Kit in place. "Tell me," he said.

Kit paused. What was the Army's interest in all this? Why were they even here? Why were three members of Weapons Research here to listen to what he had found? Could he trust them? At some level, he had little choice, but he found that he did trust them. He was proud of his country and their armed forces. Proud of their heritage and traditions. His people were followers of the Middle Way, not warmongers like the Americans or the Chinese. He would do all he could to assist them and ask nothing in return.

He explained as best he could what he had found and what he had experienced. The three weapons specialists took notes on small pads of paper, though Kit couldn't imagine what their interest was or what they were writing down.

"It goes without saying that this requires more study —*much* more study," Kit said. "We need to understand how old the substance is, and how it formed. If it has truly lasted since the Cretaceous period…"

"You have worked with a team of Americans," the colonel said. His voice was scratchy and soft. "Those Americans are here, now, in a nearby room. Do you feel their expertise would be valuable?"

Kit blinked. "They're here? Samira and Bethany and the others?"

"For the moment. They are being detained for questioning before they are deported."

He considered. Would their expertise be valuable? Of course it would. He needed *colleagues* to help him understand this problem, not soldiers and weapons experts. He needed kindred minds to test his ideas and help him come to grips with this world-shattering new discovery. This was a job for scientists. He wanted to say, *yes! Yes, bring them in!* But if the Americans came in, they would take over. It would become their project, their research. They would bring it home to the United States, to their well-stocked labs and huge grants, and use the influence of their wealth and power to rob Thailand of her history.

"No," he said. "To understand this mystery, I need the help of paleontologists and geologists and experts of every kind, but I don't need the *Americans*. Do we not have education in Thailand? Do we not have the best minds in the world? No. Give me the experts and the tools to do the job, but send the Americans away. We don't need them."

The colonel nodded, and for the first time the hint of a smile touched his fierce frown. "You shall have your experts and tools," he said. "Just tell me what you require."

AFTER THEY TOOK HIS LIST, they left Kit alone in the room with his thoughts. The view of the unfamiliar night sky in his hallucination still stuck in his mind. It had been so detailed. A brilliant spread of millions of stars, unspoiled by modern light. The surrounding foliage had been from the Cretaceous period: ferns covering the ground, and in the distance around the hill, gingkos, palms, and the tall, bare stalks of monkey puzzle trees. Of course, Kit knew what foliage would have grown in the late Cretaceous, so it wasn't unreasonable that he would hallucinate it accurately. But the sky...

He had to do it again. Foolish, probably, to intentionally breathe a substance he couldn't identify, but it hadn't hurt him the first time, had it? A little fear, perhaps, but no real harm. He couldn't analyze something scientifically with only one data point.

Carefully, Kit scraped again at the same fissure and put his face close, breathing deeply of the resulting fumes. Once again, the maniraptor appeared, beautiful and lethal and as seemingly as real as the rest of the lab. The terror hit him, too, but he resisted it this time, standing his ground, though his heart raced and his legs shook. The same hilltop presented itself to him, but this time he paid particular attention to the stars. He concentrated on two memorable clusters, trying to burn their arrangement into his memory. More quickly than he expected, the vision faded.

The moment it did, he pulled out his phone and started hunting. He remembered a website that some enterprising astronomers had put together with an interactive star chart. The site made use of the ultra-accurate star positional data produced by the Gaia space observatory to predict how the night sky would look millions of years into the past and future. After some searching, he found it and started playing with the tool, traveling back in time toward the Cretaceous period some sixty-six million years ago. As he watched, the stars orbited the galactic center in chaotic patterns, and the Earth traveled a quarter of the way around the Milky Way, utterly transforming the familiar constellations.

He started at the beginning of the Cretaceous and stepped his way forward in five million year jumps. He didn't know what time of night or season it had been, so he had to search each version of the sky in its entirety, a tedious activity, especially on his phone. He almost gave up halfway through—how could he expect to find the stars from a hallucination? He didn't know when this maniraptor had lived, even to within a few million years, and it took only thousands of years to visibly change the alignment of stars. The website couldn't even be entirely accurate that far back—the galaxy was a chaotic system, very sensitive to the accuracy of initial conditions. Millions of years was enough time for old stars to die and new ones to form.

But part of what made Kit well-suited to his profession was an inability to give up on a task, however tedious, until he had exhausted it completely. He concentrated on finding the first star cluster he had memorized: four particularly bright stars standing in a line, like Orion's belt with one extra star. The fact that he was on his phone meant he could only look at a small portion of sky at a time, but he persisted, his mind settling into the routine.

He almost didn't recognize it when he finally found it. He had reached the end of the Cretaceous and thus the end of his search, sixty-six million and forty-three thousand years ago. The date of the Chicxulub asteroid impact that had killed eighty percent of life on Earth, including most of the dinosaurs. The arrangement was upside-down on his phone from how he had seen it in the sky, but once he recognized it, there was no mistake. His four bright stars, arranged in a neat line, the second a little raised and brighter than the others and the fourth a little farther away.

He searched for the other cluster and found that one, too, slightly different than he remembered, but still recognizable. Was it possible that he'd remembered those arrangements from the first time he used the website, years earlier, and had incorporated them into his hallucination? Not likely. Not possible at all, really. But if not, that meant something even more unbelievable: that the scene he had witnessed in his hallucination was real. Those dinosaurs had actually stood on that hill, looking up at the stars. Which meant it wasn't a hallucination at all.

Kit put the phone down, breathing hard. Maybe he was just going mad. But he didn't think so. He couldn't prove it through any traditional means, but he now believed in what he had seen. Wherever that hilltop was, those maniraptors had been there. Whether intentionally or not, the event had been recorded and somehow played back to his mind all this time later. And thanks to the stars, he now knew with pinpoint accuracy when they had lived. And in all likelihood, how they had died.

CHAPTER SIX

Northeast Thailand

66 million years ago

E asy Prey tried to concentrate, but the music made it hard. The sweet-smelling love songs his coworkers preferred left an acid taste in the back of his throat. He would have used a portable facemask for his own music— Prey liked his songs pungent, with a little more rhythmic savagery in them—but Sharp Salt, his boss, had strictly forbidden personal music organisms. Ruins team unity, she said.

The data blurred a little in his nostrils. Prey hadn't been sleeping well lately, and the scent flows of astronomical data required close attention to understand properly. Normally, he was up to the task, but today, he just wanted to go home to his nest and sleep. He wondered if he was coming down with something.

He would never complain, though, no matter how bad he felt. This was a good job for a male, especially one of his caste, and he didn't want to lose it. Even for his gender, he was small, with drab plumage and a tiny wingspan. Nobody chose him for breeding. Only a mind for mathematics had set him apart and earned him a job in the sciences, surrounded by females. If he made the smallest slip, he would confirm their expectations and find himself doing manual labor for a living, like so many males his age.

A new smell cut through the music. Sharp Salt was coming.

His coworkers stepped down from their perches, capping their data flows and smoothing down their plumage. Prey had to hop down from his, which had been made for a female, and was thus too high for him to step comfortably off. The only other male in the room, Crushed Neck, began exuding sexual pheromones, a little too obviously. The females made a point of ignoring him.

Sharp Salt burst into the room along with a wash of her commanding presence. The scent filled Prey with feelings of love and devotion and duty, even though he hated her. When she was nearby, he could never disobey her. The urge to please was too strong. Anything she asked of him, he would do without question, except maybe commit suicide, and even that would take monumental willpower to resist.

Sharp Salt's full name was Sharp Salt of Ocean Spray Thrown by Morning Breakers. For a female from a prestigious Ocean roost to hold such a low leadership posting meant she must have angered someone powerful. Which perhaps explained why she was so unpleasant to those who worked for her.

Sharp Salt struck the music organism with her foot, silencing it. Prey winced. Those organisms were delicate. Too fierce a blow could break internal vessels, causing it to bruise and ultimately souring the music. Not that Prey would have minded if she just killed the thing outright.

As the music dissipated, Sharp Salt snapped her jaws and

bared a row of needle-sharp teeth. Almost immediately, an intense message scent filled Prey's nostrils, riding on the scent of Sharp Salt's presence. "I have exciting news for all of you," the message said. "Our laboratory will be visited tomorrow by distinguished leader Lush Warmth of Ocean Thermals after Rain. She has heard of your good work and wishes to breathe it in for herself."

Prey's coworkers erupted into a babble of squawks, the news surprising enough to make them forget their manners and voice their reactions instead of using scent alone. A wave of presence from Sharp Salt silenced them.

"Prey?" Sharp Salt said, using the shortest possible scent marker.

Prey's full name was Sweet Blood of Easy Prey Just After Slaughter. It was a common and forgettable name for a male. Prey wondered if his mother had actually liked it or if, in her disappointment at his gender, she had chosen the first name that occurred to her.

Prey cowered. "Yes, revered Sharp Salt of Ocean Spray Thrown by Morning Breakers?"

"Collate our most recent findings and prepare a presentation for the leader by tomorrow morning."

Prey bobbed his head in acquiescence. The job would take him all night, and Sharp Salt would be unlikely to acknowledge his hand in it to the leader. Still, she had chosen him for the job, which meant that, despite her prejudices, Sharp Salt recognized his talent. He wished that talent could serve his own advancement instead of her petty self-aggrandizement, but that was like wishing for the moon. He was a male, and males didn't rise to positions of leadership. He was lucky not to be inseminating livestock or massaging flesh into organisms in a factory somewhere.

Sharp Salt blasted a wave of sexual domination that left Prey reeling, but of course it wasn't intended for him. Crushed Neck trotted meekly out the door after her, bobbing his head and nuzzling her wing feathers. He was an admirable physical specimen, nearly as big as the females, with a brilliant red scent receptor standing out over a strong jaw. Prey suspected it was why he'd been hired. Given the quality of his work, it certainly didn't seem to be his knowledge of astrophysics.

Prey jumped back to his perch and clenched his teeth until the feeling of sexual desire had passed. No one ever wanted him for sex. His female coworkers would likely go to the breeding grounds after work and pick out a mating partner, but Prey had long since given up visiting such places. The embarrassment of being overlooked night after night left him feeling ashamed and lonely, so he spent his evenings studying astronomy, or else working late in the lab.

A FEW HOURS LATER, Prey was alone. Now that everyone else had gone, he could switch from visual mode to a full olfactory connection with the network. It took more concentration to explore the data by smell alone, but he found that the visual representations—just summaries of the scent data—tended to disguise important details and assume away outliers. A direct connection to the Ductwork served him better.

He opened a valve, and a rich melange of aromas flooded into his face. This was the Ductwork, a continuous airflow pumped through the complex of buildings that allowed computational collaboration on a large scale. Many of the big Houses performed large scale computation, but it usually meant putting hundreds or thousands of individuals into a single room or field. Females of different ranks dominated sub-groups and coordinated data flow, and at the bottom of the hierarchy, males performed the actual computations. The duration of the computation was limited by the time the males could reasonably keep working without sleep or food. With the females dominating them, that was a long time, but there were still limits.

The Ductwork was a new concept: a decentralized network that allowed computing to continue indefinitely, with shifts of males and females contributing their minds to the whole and then dropping out again. As long as they kept a minimum threshold of contributors, it didn't matter who was connected, as long as the dominating females at the top who drove the process maintained a clear purpose from shift to shift. The concept was gaining popularity, but as far as Prey knew, their House was the only one to implement it to this degree, allowing connections from anywhere in the whole complex of buildings.

Some intellectuals had discussed the possibility that *multiple* Houses could connect in this fashion, allowing collaboration on an unprecedented scale. More radical thinkers pushed the thought further, imagining networks without domination, where each participant contributed towards a consensus goal rather than one given by decree from the top. Such a network could conceivably operate without any females at all. Personally, Prey thought it was more likely to devolve into chaos than accomplish anything practical, but he liked the idea of it. A group of males achieving something on their own, with no females! It was an exciting time to be alive.

He exuded scent into the Ductwork, announcing himself with his unique scent marker and declaring himself as an analytical adjunct. This allowed him to filter out the command scents and perform computations on the data instead becoming a direct part of the computational engine himself. Analysis was traditionally done by females, so he occasionally had problems with female leadership denying him access, but no one stopped him today.

He began sifting through the latest astronomy data. Ever since Thick Loam of Forest Rich with Spring Growth had discovered an eighth planetary body in their solar system,

Ocean Roost had doubled its astronomical research efforts, trying not to lose prestige to the Forest Roost. At the upper levels of roost politics, prestige was power, and those with the most could sway lesser roosts to follow their lead. Sharp Salt wanted Prey to summarize the latest findings, especially anything that might hint at new breakthrough discoveries to be made.

They had recently discovered a new moon around the sixth planet, but so many of those had been discovered by now that they had ceased to be particularly prestigious. They wanted something new, something spectacular. So Prey scoured the data, summarizing the tracking of thousands of asteroids, looking for orbital anomalies that might imply the existence of a larger body previously overlooked.

He worked for hours before he found it, and when he did, he could hardly believe what he saw. He double-checked the computations and got the same results. A chill went down his spine from his neck to the tip of his tail. This wasn't possible. Nothing like this had ever been found, though given the cratered appearance of the moon, the idea had certainly been considered. Either this discovery would mean immense prestige for Ocean Roost, or else...he needed to refine the measurements. The precision of the data wasn't nearly good enough for what he needed.

Prey hopped down from his perch, fluffed his feathers to get some circulation moving again, and headed outside to visit the telescope.

He left the building and hopped to the top of the hill, beyond which a cliff dropped to a sandy beach below. At the top, spread out in a hexagonal pattern, stood four hundred males, looking at the sky. Together, the males formed the largest telescope Ocean Roost had ever formed, possibly the largest formed by any roost. All of them had been bioengineered to give them extraordinary eyesight. Females were never modified—most would have considered it immoral—

but males and animals often were to make them more useful to the community.

Dozens of other males climbed the hill and walked through the configuration, finding their places. It was shift change, each male finishing a ten-hour rotation before being replaced by a new one in the same location on the hill. Prey scanned the crowd for Soft Meat, a friend from his school days. They had studied astronomy and mathematics together, though Meat had not risen as high afterward.

Prey smelled his friend's marker and triangulated on him in the crowd. Meat looked exhausted, having just finished his own shift. When Prey called him, he responded slowly, a little dazed by having complete control of his own mind again.

"Meat!" Prey addressed him verbally, using the low-caste language mostly used by males. It had less range of expression and less precision than communicating by smell, but it had the advantage that most females couldn't understand it. He knocked his jaw affectionately against his friend's. "We need to talk."

They stepped to the edge of the configuration, looking down on the ocean. A cool breeze ruffled their feathers, and as Prey talked, the hazy look in Meat's eyes started to clear. Meat was a talented mathematician, wasted as a simple computer node. If he'd been female, he would be running his own lab by now.

"Are you sure?" Meat asked, wide awake now. "How precise is the data?"

"Not nearly precise enough."

"But if you're right..."

"We need to know, and we need to know as soon as possible. Help me."

Meat, realizing what Prey wanted to do, bared his teeth and exuded a negation—a scent that coming from a female would compel obedience, but from Meat just expressed disagreement. "You can't," he said. "You'll get us both evicted from the roost. Wait until morning and let Sharp Salt decide."

"That's hours wasted," Prey said. "And what if she doesn't believe me? Or decides to bury it and hope for the best rather than bring bad news to her superiors?"

"It's not like we can do anything about it even if it's true."

"Maybe not. But we can't even try if we don't know."

Prey didn't wait for Meat to answer. He turned around and walked to the center of the configuration, where he started exuding scent. There would be a female somewhere in the building who was remotely controlling the telescope, her scent commands telling each of them how to focus and how and where to scan. Prey couldn't dominate the males himself, but as a member of Sharp Salt's team, he could invoke her authority. He did that now, exuding *her* scent marker and telling them that by her authority they had a new target to follow. The goal: as precise a prediction of location and trajectory as possible.

As each of the males stared at the same spot in the sky, they translated the light gathered by each of them into smell. The smells were then synthesized mathematically to simulate the result of a single, giant lens the size of the entire circle of males. The technique had only been developed in the last several years. Before that, astronomy had relied on manufactured organisms like giant eyes and multiple lenses arranged in an exoskeleton. The bigger the eye, the farther one could see, but the manufacturers had reached a limit for how large such organisms could be grown.

The four hundred males on the hilltop adjusted their position, shrinking the telescope by drawing closer to each other. This decreased the aperture of the lens, but increased its resolution. Together they focused on the spot of sky that Prey indicated. He hoped they had enough time. The longer they could track the object, the more precise their estimate would be. Eventually, though, the female in the building would realize that the males weren't following her commands, and then they would be finished.

The calculations were complex, and he had to guide them through it. Meat stayed and helped, working the more difficult bits himself and farming out the rest. The basic approach was familiar to most of the males there: Each object in space pulled on others that passed nearby, perturbing their orbit. If a known orbit deviated slightly, that meant an unknown object had flown by and influenced it. By recognizing such anomalies in multiple known orbits, they could predict the orbits of objects that were too small to see directly, like following broken branches through a forest to locate prey.

Only it was much more complicated than that. Even well-known objects followed irregular paths if you looked closely enough. The masses they orbited weren't perfectly spherical or uniformly dense, causing jitters and jags. That made it difficult to tease out the normal variations from the abnormal ones. It wasn't impossible, but it required high precision, and that took time.

They worked for an hour, then two. The female tasked with dominating the telescope must not have been paying very close attention. Females relegated to night shift computing would be those whose careers had shown little promise, however, and the job amounted to little more than commands to keep working. Perhaps they were accustomed to ignoring the output.

As the results of their calculations began to take shape, a ripple passed through the crowd of males. Although their minds were slaved to the computational task, they retained enough individual awareness to understand the nature of the orbit their calculations were gradually refining. To follow the path it struck through the cosmos. And to see what it intersected.

A sudden ferocious sensation tore through him, ripping his mind out of the network. Three females had come up behind him. They flooded him with scent, a domination strong enough to be punitive. All thought of resistance fled. Prey fell to the ground and groveled, flattening his tail and scraping his face in the dirt. The other males around him whimpered and abased themselves, cowed by the scent even though it was linked to Prey's marker and directed at him. The telescope fell apart.

Prey urinated reflexively, showing his deference. He was at their mercy now, but they had been too slow. The computation had completed, or near enough, and his suspicions had been confirmed. He felt a mix of elation and terror at the prospect.

"You will not move," the scent commanded. "You will not speak. Sharp Salt of Ocean Spray Thrown by Morning Breakers will know of this."

Prey stared at the dirt and imagined the object hurtling along in its trajectory, unstoppable. *Everyone will know of this.*

CHAPTER SEVEN

Their classroom prison cell grew dark as night fell. Arun and Gabby curled up against each other and seemed to find some restless sleep, but Samira stared out into the darkness, wide awake. Her mind played back the image of the smashed fossils in an unrelenting loop. Beth lay on her back nearby, staring at the ceiling.

"I've read about situations like this," Beth said. "Americans trapped in foreign countries when the government crashes. It never turns out well."

"Those are just the cases they write about," Samira said. "You don't hear about the people who get back home easy."

"I think it's too late for easy."

Samira's mind flashed yet again on the scattered destruction of plaster and fossilized bone. Would it be possible to piece it back together again? Would they even get a chance to try? She gripped her hair with both hands and pulled hard, letting out a groan of frustration.

Beth sat up. "Come here," she said, beckoning.

Samira shifted and slid backward along the floor until she felt Beth's hands take hold of her hair and twist it gently, running her fingers through and loosening the braid. The motion soothed her, calming her breathing and settling her heart rate. It sent her back to their shared room in Ethiopia when they were girls, the warm night air drifting through the open window, the smell of smoke from the compound fires, the tinkling sound of tiny bells, and the lilting chant of evening prayers. Beth pulled her hair taut and rebraided it quickly with strong fingers, little tugs that pulled her head side to side. When she was done, they swapped places, and Samira did the same in return. It was a ritual, regularly practiced as children, but rare now.

It was only with Beth sitting in front of her that Samira realized that her sister's body was shaking. "Hey," Samira said, squeezing her shoulders. "Hey, it's going to be all right. They can't keep us here for long. We haven't done anything wrong."

"But if they think we're spies…"

"No. These people aren't hostage-takers; they'll see there's no advantage in keeping us here."

Samira realized Gabby was awake and watching them. "I don't actually know the story of you two," Gabby said. "I mean, Ethiopia, missionary kids, adoption: got it. But not the story."

"Not much to tell," Samira said.

"Dad was an opthamologist," Beth said. "Pretty rare in Ethiopia in those days, pretty rare even now. Thousands of people living with treatable blindness due to cataracts, trachoma, uveitis." She stopped there, not wanting to share more of the story than Samira was comfortable with. Samira didn't like to get into the details, and Beth knew it. At the moment, though, any distraction was welcome.

"I grew up in a small village in the mountains, far from anything," Samira said. "I had juvenile cataracts, and I'd lost most of my vision. My mother decided to bring me to the clinic, probably a hundred miles from home, and farther away than she'd ever been. She died on the way. I made my way to the clinic alone."

"How old were you?"

"I was six."

The room fell quiet, with only the soft sound of Samira still braiding Beth's hair. Samira couldn't remember her father, couldn't even identify the village she had come from. She didn't know which of the many possible health conditions had claimed her mother's life. But six years old and nearly blind, she had somehow followed the road to the clinic.

"And Beth's parents adopted you?" Gabby asked.

"Eventually."

This was the part Samira avoided discussing. It was a problematic narrative, a cliche almost: the white savior restoring the sight of the black orphan child and lifting her out of poverty. Samira had spent a lot of her life trying not to be defined by that myth. Part of what made that hard was that Beth's father seemed to define himself by it. Mom and Dad had given up everything to come to Africa—family and friends, the comforts of home, the money Dad could have made as an opthamologist in the US—and they literally brought sight to the blind, like a Biblical miracle. For Dad, it was the fulfillment of his life's calling.

And yes, they had sacrificed to come, and the work they did was good and important, a work few doctors were willing to cross the world to do. To the Ethiopians, however, the Americans were still the richest people in town—in any of the surrounding towns—and the idea of being grateful to them for giving up even greater riches would never have occurred to them. For the hundreds who stood in line in the baking sun, waiting to be treated, the Americans were simply the ones who had everything.

It hadn't been easy for Samira, growing up as the Ethiopian daughter of the white American *faringe*. She never really fit in either culture. She knew the language and food and customs of her adopted family, but her skin matched the others at school and in their neighborhood. Beth had grown up with a similar disconnect, though her skin was as white as the goat's milk they bought every day from the woman on the corner. Despite her color, Beth knew the music and games and food of Ethiopia, spoke Amharic as easily as English, and thought it was normal to have cows and chickens and occasionally even a hyena wandering the streets in front of their house. She and Samira were what sociologists called Third Culture Kids: influenced by two different cultures, but really just in a third culture of their own.

Gabby didn't press for more details, and eventually both she and Beth drifted into restless sleep stretched out on the floor. Samira leaned her back against the wall, thinking of all the countries she had visited over the years. All the conferences throughout Africa and India that her father had attended, family in tow, to speak about African medical missions. The trips to Argentina and China and Poland and Spain as a grad student learning field paleontology. She had seen most of the corners of the world, but none of them felt like home. She and Beth rented an apartment together in Colorado, but it was just a place to sleep, not a place she belonged. She wondered if she would ever truly belong anywhere.

When the early light of day filtered through the grimy window, Samira still hadn't slept.

THE OTHERS JOLTED awake when the door flew open. A guard pointed his weapon around the room, presumably to make sure they weren't hiding behind the door to ambush him. The colonel strode in behind him.

"You are free to go," he said. "My men will escort you to Suvarnabhumi Airport and see you onto your plane."

Samira stood. "Free?" she said. "You've held us for no

reason and stolen and destroyed our work. You expect us to be grateful?"

Beth put a hand on her shoulder. "Sami."

"Your transportation is your own problem," the colonel said. "Be grateful you are allowed the opportunity."

"I'm not leaving without our fossils," Samira said. "You wrecked them, but we might still be able to learn some—"

"Yours?" the colonel demanded. He stepped close and thrust his face into hers. "You come to Thailand and dig fossils out of our ground, then presume to call them *yours*?"

"Come on, let's go while we still can," Beth said, tugging on her arm.

"Listen to her and go before I change my mind," the colonel said.

Samira didn't actually think he could change his mind. Judging by his face, the instruction to let them go had likely come from a superior, and he would have held them longer if it were up to him. But she doubted she could talk him into giving up the broken fossils. She remembered Beth's advice and decided not to put him in a situation where he had to harm them in some fresh way in order to save face.

She bowed her head slightly. "We will leave now."

THE FLIGHT HOME WAS INTERMINABLE. Trying to sleep in coach was like one of those tortures where they put someone in a box that's too small to stand, sit, or lie down in comfortably. Beth could curl her legs up underneath her and slept soundly, but Samira, though she leaned the seat back as far as it would go and covered her eyes, could never quite manage it. Eventually, she gave up and watched endless in-flight movies that all blurred together in her increasingly muddled brain. Twenty-six hours later, after a brief layover in

Tokyo, they landed in Chicago with only a two-hour flight left to reach Denver.

She waited in the customs line with her baggage, feeling angry at the world. There was no logical reason whatsoever why they needed to be thrown out of Thailand. What did it have to do with her what country controlled the South China Sea? Couldn't they resolve that without interfering with her work? It killed her to think of all those maniraptors, possibly the greatest find of the century, lying inaccessible to her on the other side of the world. And when she thought of the fossils they had spent the season carefully excavating a millimeter at a time, smashed and scattered on the gymnasium floor, she wanted to vomit. The knowledge they could have gained from those bones was priceless, and might be lost forever.

She had heard Americans describe the sense of coming home they felt when they reached customs and could walk past the line of tourists to the expedited "US Citizens" lane. As a citizen, Samira could do the same, but despite her years of living there, the United States didn't feel like home. She felt a nervous tension instead, expecting at any moment to be turned away. If a customs official had given her a hard time today, she might have punched him.

The checks were more thorough than she remembered, and posted signs warned that anyone feeling sick should ask to see the staff nurse before entering the country. Apparently a particularly virulent disease had claimed some lives in Argentina, and more cases had shown up in Uruguay and Brazil. Airports were on alert, and she was asked several times if she'd visited any of those countries.

They eventually passed through and endured the short flight to Denver. When she finally walked out of the airport with her bags, she told Beth she would see her at the apartment later. She knew she should go home and get some sleep, but when she climbed into the taxi outside the airport, she told the man to drive her to the University of Colorado instead. She'd been missing Wallace long enough, and she wasn't going to wait a moment longer than necessary to see him again.

THE BOULDER CAMPUS shone like a postcard. The greens and yellows of the trees and the red roofs of the buildings glowed brilliant in the sunshine as the brown foothills of the Rockies behind them rose up into the blue sky. The white peaks visible from Denver were obscured here; in a quirk of geography, as one approached the foothills, the mountains seemed to sink until they disappeared behind the ridge. The Ornithology Center stood in the shadow of the football stadium, a shiny new building that had become one of the university's claims to fame. As she approached, she saw that it was public viewing hours for Lewis.

A small crowd gathered around the fenced area, mostly tourists rather than students. Samira stopped by the fence to see. Lewis was out, as unperturbed by the crowd as always, pecking at a ripe mango in his food dish.

Lewis was a dodo. The only dodo to draw breath on planet Earth for nearly four hundred years. Possibly the most famous of the many animal species eradicated by humanity, dodos had been wiped out by seventeenth century sailors who had hunted it to extinction on its island home of Mauritius, near Madagascar. If not for modern science, and for a dried head saved for centuries in the Oxford University museum collection, no one would ever have seen a living dodo again.

It looked like a giant pigeon. About three feet tall, it had brownish-gray feathers, stubby wings, and a naked head like a buzzard's. It was, in short, an ugly bird, one likely to be passed over quickly by zoo-goers if they didn't know what it was. Extinction had given Lewis celebrity status.

Lewis was not the first animal to be brought back from

extinction. That distinction belonged to a Pyrenean ibex that had been revived from frozen cells in a laboratory in Spain in 2003. The ibex had died shortly after birth, but years later, a passenger pigeon named Bruce was genetically engineered from sequenced DNA and lived for five years. Bruce became a worldwide celebrity, prompting a revolution in funding for de-extinction projects, including Queequeg the Quagga, Charlotte the Tasmanian wolf, and a dozen or so gastric-brooding frogs that, to Beth's knowledge, had never been named.

When Lewis was born, he was by far the oldest species to be brought back from extinction, the last dodo before him having died in 1662. His record had been eclipsed several months ago, however, when a surrogate Asian elephant mother in Massachusetts successfully gave birth to a woolly mammoth calf named George.

George wasn't truly a mammoth, despite his large size and substantial pelt of hair. No fully-intact mammoth DNA had survived the four thousand years since the last of the species had died. Instead, Dr. Church and his team took the broken bits they could extract from several frozen carcasses and solved the world's largest jigsaw puzzle, using elephant DNA to fill in the gaps. The result was an elephant-mammoth hybrid, still an impressive feat of genetic engineering, but not technically the same creature that had roamed the Siberian tundra.

Samira watched the ungainly dodo hop around its pen, marveling that such a thing had become possible in her lifetime. They might never see dinosaurs walking the Earth again —sixty-six million years was a great deal more time for DNA to survive than four thousand, even if trapped in amber—but to be able to reclaim species that were recently lost was an incredible thing.

Lewis approached the fence, showing the same lack of fear of humans that his ancestors had shown when sailors discovered their island and began slaughtering them to fill their ship larders with fresh meat. It gave every impression of fitting the fat, stupid stereotype of its kind, although Samira knew research had shown it to be reasonably intelligent, along the lines of a modern Canada goose. Not being afraid of humans wasn't a problem of intellect. Its species had just never had the experience to teach it otherwise.

"He's a beauty, in his own way," said a voice behind her.

Samira turned to see a short, egg-shaped woman with deep creases at the corners of her eyes and a pleasant smile.

"Paula!"

Paula Shapiro flapped her short arms, looking a bit like a dodo herself. "Samira. Come here, my dear. Give us a hug."

Samira stepped gratefully into the older woman's warm embrace, feeling the stress of the last week melt somewhat. In Paula's care, it seemed like everything would be all right.

Dr. Paula Shapiro ruled the avian lab at the University of Colorado like a mother bird, taking graduate students under her wing like chicks to nurture to adulthood. She baked cookies and cupcakes, remembered her students' birthdays, and seemed to sense immediately whenever one of them was hurting or needed to talk. She treated her birds and her graduate students more or less the same, with the same tone of voice and loving concern. Heaven help the student who mistreated one or the other, though. Paula would kick them out of the nest as quickly and ruthlessly as many mother birds did to young that didn't measure up.

Paula knew more about avian genetics and behavior than most people alive. She was an anatomist, a rare and vanishing breed in an age of computerized statistical modeling. She worked with living dinosaurs in order to understand the extinct ones, and had pioneered some of the techniques that had made it possible for Lewis to be hatched from a Nicobar pigeon egg. Samira had studied with her before getting her doctorate and becoming a professor in her own right, but even now, Paula held a special place in her heart.

"I hear you had a rough time in Thailand," Paula said. "Why don't you come inside and tell me about it."

Five minutes later, Samira found herself in Paula's office, eating homemade shortbread cookies and sipping tea—always tea, never coffee, in delicate, flowered tea cups—and spilling the whole sad story.

"They seemed to think we were spies or something. They were very suspicious about the CIA funding we got, though as far as I can tell, it was totally innocent. And then"—it was hard to say, even now—"they destroyed our fossils. Just tore into them with crowbars, as if we were hiding something." She could see the demolished pieces in her mind's eye, the chunks of plaster littering the gymnasium floor, the scraped and broken bones. Even then, if they'd been allowed to take them home, they could probably have learned something from them, despite the contamination of the data. But they hadn't even been allowed that much.

Paula listened carefully, her expression sympathetic and intent. She was not one for drama or bursts of emotion, but Samira could see the rage smoldering in her eyes. There was nothing Paula cared about more than advancing knowledge of extinct avian species, unless it was taking care of the species we still had left.

"Which brings me to the guy from the CIA," Samira said.

Paula met her eye and nodded. *Of course it does.* Her gaze didn't waver, but Samira caught a look of—could it be guilt? —in Paula's expression.

"Beth said it was you who passed that contact on to her," Samira continued. "And though of course I'm grateful, I can't help wondering now...do you know who in the CIA I could talk to? If we were being played in some way, I'd like to know why."

Paula stood and bustled over to the hotpot to pour another cup. Samira noticed how much older she seemed, her face more deeply wrinkled, and her movements stiff and careful. It occurred to her that Paula was probably past retirement age, and might reasonably be expected to throw in the towel before long. The thought startled and horrified her.

"Sit down," Samira said. "I can get that."

"Oh, I'm fine, I'm fine." Paula waved her away. "It's just my hip. They say I'll need a replacement soon, but I'd rather wait as long as I can." She turned back with the tea and grinned. "It's always the hips that are causing problems, isn't it?"

It was a dinosaur joke. Dinosaurs had traditionally been divided into two primary categories according to their hips: saurischian, or "lizard-hipped," and ornithischian, or "bird-hipped." In recent years, this phylogeny had come under some criticism, not least of which because modern birds had clearly evolved from the *lizard-hipped* branch. The hip controversy had produced dozens of new organizational proposals and more than one bar fight at international conventions.

"Our find might have shed some light on that," Samira said. "It might have shed light on a lot of things."

She hadn't yet mentioned the unbelievable part of their discovery. She had skipped from the packing up of three partial skeletons of a new maniraptoran species to their arrest by the Thai military and the confiscation and destruction of their finds. The story was wild enough without adding the possibility that these particular maniraptors had held funeral services and buried their dead. As much as she trusted Paula, and as much as she wanted to tell her, Samira knew her career could suffer badly if this idea got out without the evidence to back it up.

"It was Dan Everson who contacted you, right?" Paula asked. "From the Agency, I mean?"

Samira laughed. "Do you hang out with a lot of CIA agents?"

"No, he's the one I know," Paula said, and once again Samira caught that expression—a slight wince, as if Paula felt guilty about what she was saying. "If you can call it knowing. He's contributed funds to my research more than once. He expressed interest in yours, and I gave him your number. But I didn't know if it had been him or some other agent who made the connection."

Samira sipped her tea and sighed. "It seems so ridiculous. The CIA, sponsoring my research. Like a James Bond movie or something."

"I'm sorry I passed them on to you," Paula said. "I had no idea it would cause so many problems."

She ducked her head slightly to take another sip of tea. Maybe she just felt guilty that her recommendation might have indirectly caused problems, but Samira got the distinct impression that Paula was lying, or at least not sharing everything she knew. Odd.

"Well, here I am gabbing at you when you must be anxious to see Wallace," Paula said. She retrieved Samira's teacup and cookie plate and set them on the counter. "I'm a little surprised he hasn't figured out you're here and started calling for you."

Samira stood, setting her suspicions aside. Wallace was the reason she'd come, after all, and she missed him terribly. She was lucky to have someone like Paula to watch him while she was out of the country. She didn't know anyone else she would have trusted to care for him, which could have been a real problem for her career.

She followed Paula further back into the lab, where the coos and warbles and squawks of the avian lab became audible. They rounded a corner to find a cockatoo standing on top of his open cage.

"You bastard," the cockatoo said.

Samira smiled. "Hey, Mikey. Life treating you well?"

"Hello. Hello. Go to hell," the bird replied.

Mikey had been a rescue, and had a colorful vocabulary. He didn't mean anything by it; he was simply repeating the songs he'd learned from his flock. His flock just happened to be two teenage boys whose mother had purchased the bird as a pet without realizing how much care and attention such a pet required. Fortunately, he hadn't been as mistreated or neglected as some shelter birds, so he hadn't become violent. A cockatoo could easily break a human finger with its beak, so if he'd shown any signs of aggression, he would have been kept in his cage.

Paula reached out a hand, and Mikey briefly nuzzled her, rubbing the short feathers of his neck against her wrist. "That's a good bird," she said.

"Screw you," Mikey said, affectionately.

Most of the larger birds in the lab roamed free during the day, unless the requirements of research or their care didn't allow it. Some rarely left the comforts of their cages even when the doors were open. A baby scarlet macaw was one of the few enclosed; it slept peacefully, snuggled up with a soft scrap of blanket and clutching a mangled stuffed bear.

In one corner, a raven stood on the floor, watching an animated children's program on an old television. Its gleaming black body bobbed right and left as the manic characters raced from one end of the screen to the other. "Marcy would watch that garbage all day long if I let her," Paula said. "She's as bad as a toddler."

Even over the general din, they heard Wallace's squawks long before they reached the back of the room. He had seen Samira coming and was letting the world know it.

A brilliant red-and-green macaw, Wallace stood on a wooden perch made to resemble a small tree. When Samira held out her arm to him, he pushed her away with his head. When she did it a second time, he pecked her—not enough to draw blood, which he was certainly capable of, but enough to show his displeasure.

"He's cross with you," Paula said.

"Oh, come on, Wallace," Samira said. "I came back,

didn't I? And I left you with Auntie Paula and all your friends here."

Wallace squawked loud enough to make her wince.

"Well, fine then, you can stay here." She turned to leave, but as she did, she pulled a package of peanut butter crackers out of her pocket and pulled open the plastic wrapper. "I was going to give you this, but..."

With an inelegant flutter, he left his perch and landed on her shoulder, where he gave her a sharp rap on the top of her head. Samira laughed and handed him a cracker, which Wallace accepted gravely, head held high.

"You should never have let him get in that habit," Paula said, meaning the shoulder perch, not the cracker. Standing on her shoulders meant Wallace's head was higher than hers, which in bird society meant he was her superior. "You're just letting him think he's the alpha bird."

"I know," Samira said. "But shoulder or not, he's in charge, and he knows it. I can't say no to him. Besides, I like him there."

Wallace knocked his beak against her head, more gently this time, and she offered up another cracker.

"Yep, he's got you trained," Paula said.

Samira thanked Paula profusely for letting Wallace stay— she hadn't even charged for his care. Before she left, however, she had one more question.

"How intelligent do you think birds could really get?"

Paula looked startled at first, then gave Samira a searching stare. "You know how much Wallace can understand."

"As a pet owner, sure. But nobody knows living birds like you do. Besides, I'm just looking for an opinion. Birds have no corpus callosum connecting the halves of their brains. Could they ever reach the intelligence level of great apes? Or humans? If they did, what might it look like?"

"Birds are already as smart as the great apes," Paula said. "Some of them are, anyway."

"Come on. That's a bit biased, don't you think?"

"You asked for my opinion; I gave it."

"But chimpanzees have learned hundreds of words of sign language. They can build tools, anticipate the future, show self-control for a greater reward."

"African grays have learned to speak hundreds of phrases. Not just to parrot them back—if you pardon the expression—but using them with meaning to ask for what they want or to express a feeling. Ravens not only use tools; they store useful ones because they think they might need them again later."

"Still…"

"Come with me." Paula turned and marched back into the bird room, leaving Samira to follow. "The problem is that bird intelligence is alien to us. We *are* great apes, so the emotions and problem solving skills of apes are familiar to us. When was the last time you heard of a great ape—or a human for that matter—who could navigate from Canada to Argentina and back again, and then land in the same bush they started from? And yet, even relatively small-brained birds manage that feat every year."

When they approached his cage, Wallace squawked and dug his feet into Samira's shoulder. "See?" Paula said. "He thinks ahead. He's afraid you're going to leave him here again."

They stopped at the back of the room where Marcy the raven still watched television avidly. A young man stood at a sink nearby, rinsing bird poop off of the plastic bottom of a cage. He was tall and exceptionally thin, with unruly brown hair that fell in his face.

"Trevor, could you get me Marcy's keys?"

The young man flicked his head to sweep the hair out of his eyes, turned off the sink, and dried his hands on a towel. "Sure, you want her puzzle box, too?"

"No, just the keys, please, and a few crackers."

Trevor wandered off to do as Paula asked. Samira remembered filling the same role, years ago, working under Paula in the lab, cleaning the cages and feeding the birds and participating in her experiments. Trevor returned with a package of peanut butter crackers and a ring of small metal keys.

"Marcy's quite fond of peanut butter, just like Wallace," Paula said. "There's a box in her cage that we put crackers in, but the box requires a key. When she's good, we give her a key, and later, in the evening, we put crackers in the box and she can open it and have a treat. If she loses the key, she has no way to open the box, so she has to keep track of it."

Paula pulled a peanut butter cracker from the package and maneuvered a key off of the ring. "Watch." She gave the key to Trevor, and the two of them knelt on opposite sides of the raven, Paula holding out the cracker and Trevor holding out the key. The raven cocked its head, looking first at one and then the other.

"We've done this before, so she understands she will only get one of these things," Paula said. "Either the immediate reward of the cracker, or the larger eventual reward that the key represents."

Samira watched the raven consider its choice. Its black, emotionless eyes gave no hint of its thoughts, and she thought: *it's alien, all right.* The raven darted for Trevor and scooped up the key. Paula closed her hand around the cracker and stood, slipping it back into her pocket. The raven flapped twice to reach its cage and ducked inside to hide the key there.

"But that's just association," Samira objected. "You've given Marcy a strong positive association with the key, so she picks the key over the cracker. It doesn't mean she's thinking it through and making plans about the future."

"Sure it does," Paula said. "Watch."

When the raven returned, Paula took the cracker out of her pocket again and handed Trevor another key from the ring. They both knelt again and offered the bird the same choice. This time, Marcy didn't hesitate. She snatched the cracker and gobbled it down. Paula stood with a triumphant smile.

"She already has a key to open the box," Paula said. "She knows she doesn't need another one."

SAMIRA LEFT with Wallace proudly erect on her shoulder. Lewis the dodo hopped around his cage, flapping his wings uselessly, as they passed. Was it possible? Had there really been a race of avian dinosaurs with intelligence to rival *homo sapiens?* Or was her mind jumping to unwarranted conclusions based on the neat placement of skeletons in the ground? Maybe it was just a curious animal behavior rather than an indication of self-awareness and civilization.

But Samira didn't think so. She wasn't ready to give up on the mystery just because she'd been thrown out of Thailand, either. Somebody knew more than they were saying, and she needed to find out what. The first step was to call Dan Everson of the CIA.

CHAPTER EIGHT

The day after Kit discovered the green chemical, the Royal Thai Army invaded Sirindhorn Museum. Whatever need for secrecy or discretion had held the colonel back before, he had apparently changed his mind. Twenty military trucks poured into the parking lot and uniformed and armored soldiers jumped out. They surged down the tiled path between statues of sauropods and hadrosaurs. A few minutes later, a stream of tourists, some worried, some annoyed, streamed out of the doors and headed for their cars. Soldiers in the courtyard directed them, explaining in Thai and in English that an anonymous bomb threat had been received and the facility had to be closed for their safety.

Sirindhorn Museum had been named for Princess Maha Chakri Sirindhorn, daughter of the previous king. The princess had championed science and technology in Thailand, promoting education and research and education for women, and as a result many of the major scientific institutions of Thailand—and even a few species of dinosaur—were named after her. She had no children, but she had left one more namesake: her great-grandniece had been named in her honor. Now twenty-eight years old, the younger Princess Sirindhorn had captured the people's hearts and carried on her spirit. The princess spent her time and fortune as an activist, campaigning against the rampant sex trafficking trade and promoting women's rights. Someday, Kit thought, when he had accomplished something great for Thailand, he would meet her, and his life would be complete. He imagined the young princess pinning an award to his shirt and smiling at him in respect and admiration...

"Come," the colonel said, snapping Kit out of his fantasy. As they walked into the museum, the soldiers parted like sliding doors to let them pass. The gray exterior of the building had no ornament save the name of the museum in silver letters, both in flowing Thai characters and blocky English text. Inside, however, the main hall rose three stories past viewing balconies to a glass dome. Large dinosaur skeletons dominated the space, most reproductions of fossils discovered in Thailand. Kit recognized Compsognathus and Psittacosaurus and Siamotyrannus, each arranged in a pose of violent activity. The room throbbed with bright colors, every available wall covered with cartoonish explanations of dinosaur life and evolution. There was an earthen smell, like an underground cellar.

"This way, sir," a lieutenant said, and the colonel and Kit followed him across the main viewing area, down a narrow hallway, and out a back door into a small courtyard. They crossed the courtyard into another building, which they entered through glass doors.

The research facility had none of the glitz of the museum. The walls were bare and gray. The soldiers' boots echoed on concrete floors as the lieutenant led them down another hallway to the preparation room. Now *this* was a proper paleontology lab. The place had a warehouse feel, with a high ceiling, exposed beams, and a yellow concrete floor. He counted twelve stations arranged in pairs, each pair equipped with a microscope on a boom arm, an air compressor, and an array of neatly organized preparation tools. Plaster-encased fossils sat waiting their turn on the tables, and rows of trays held carefully extracted and polished bones.

A line of white-lab-coated scientists and technicians stood against the back wall, most of them looking terrified of the armed soldiers who had invaded their workplace. All except one: a young woman, tall for a Thai, her dark hair swept back in a neat ponytail, refused to leave her post near the front of the room. She stood with feet planted and fists on her hips, her chin held high, informing a young soldier in angry, rapid Thai that he had no right to invade her lab or bully her into submission.

"Hello, Arinya." Kit said.

She whirled at the sound of her name. Spotting him, she stalked past the soldier toward him. "Kit! Are you behind this?" she demanded.

Under her lab coat, Arinya wore a dark purple blouse made of some shiny material and a light scarf of the same color. A thin gold necklace with a single diamond hung against her throat. Makeup accentuated her dark eyes, which were flashing with barely-contained fury.

"Behind this?" Kit gave an embarrassed laugh of surprise. "They won't even tell me what's going on."

"But you're working for them?"

He was, of course, but he suddenly felt ashamed to admit it. "They took my specimens and I came along. I don't know anything more than you do."

She turned to the colonel. "I guess that means you're in charge. This is a public museum and scientific institution. By what right do you turn away our guests and disrupt our work? You have no jurisdiction here."

The colonel regarded her with cold eyes and an empty expression. "Young lady, you will find that I have jurisdiction over a great many things. This is a federal institution. This museum, and your place in it, continues by the grace of His Majesty the King. You are welcome to try pitting your contacts in high government against mine, but I assure you, mine are better."

Her eyes narrowed. "What do you want?"

"I want to use your facilities. And I want you out of the building." He cocked his head at a waiting soldier, who moved to take her arm.

"Wait," Kit said. "This is Dr. Arinya Tavaranan. We need her."

The colonel turned his flat gaze on Kit. "Why?"

"You asked if we needed the Americans, and I said no, we have all the experts we need in Thailand. But she is one of those experts. We need her to make sense of what I saw."

"I'm not working for you," she said. "No way. You might be able to shut us down, but you can't make me help you."

"Arinya—"

"No! I don't know how he bought you off, but this isn't how it works. The government gives research grants; they don't barge in with guns and demand lab time. It smells. I want no part of it."

"You don't even know what we found."

"Would it make a difference?"

He pitched his voice low, although why, he wasn't sure. "It's big, Arinya."

"And if you tell me, then they won't let me leave. No thank you."

Kit reached into his pocket and pulled out a tiny snap-shut plastic case from the boxes of dentistry equipment. He suspected the cases were meant to hold dentures, but he had repurposed them as sample cases. He opened it and held it out to Arinya. "Just take a look," he said.

"What is this?" she asked, but as he expected, she couldn't resist looking. He had put some scrapings from the dried green liquid into the case.

"I was hoping you could tell me," he said. "It oozed up out of a fissure in a Cretaceous fossil we found near Khai Nun."

"If it was still liquid, it couldn't be that old," she said. She peered closer, which as Kit had hoped, brought her close enough to smell it. She wrinkled her nose at first, then gasped, then shouted and backed away, dropping the case. Kit, expecting her reaction, deftly caught it and closed it again, returning it to his pocket. Arinya backed against the wall, her jaw moving, eyes wild. She slid down the wall to the floor. A moment later, she looked up, and Kit knew she was seeing the stars.

It was strange to see someone else experiencing it. From inside the hallucination, it had seemed to take much longer. When her vision cleared, he crouched next to her, talking fast. "It's a real Cretaceous sky," he said. "I checked. Sixty-six million years ago. That scene…it's a recording of some kind. It really happened. They were really there."

Her eyes took a moment to focus, and when they did, they focused on him. With a shout, she pushed him over. He landed ungracefully on his backside. She scrambled to her feet. "You did that on purpose. You tricked me."

"You had to see. I knew if you saw it, there's no way you could leave it behind."

"I hardly have a choice now, do I?" She threw an arm toward where the colonel watched them, impassive. "He's not going to let me just waltz away now that you've brought me in on the secret."

"You may leave if you wish," the colonel said. "I'm no jailer. But if you do, it's with the understanding that you will tell no one. Not the press, not your colleagues from other nations, not even your husband."

"I don't have a husband."

"Not one person. If you do, I will have you arrested for espionage and held for interrogation in a dark hole for a very long time."

She held his gaze. "I thought you weren't a jailer."

"Not unless I have to be."

She crossed her arms across the front of her lab coat. "Why do you care? These creatures, whatever the truth about them, are millions of years dead. They're hardly a threat to national security."

"That is not your affair," the colonel said. "Are you in or are you out?"

She held his eyes for another beat, then shook her head and looked at Kit, who still sat on the floor where she'd pushed him. "You're a real bastard, you know that?"

He climbed to his feet. "Does that mean you're in?"

"You really pulled that stuff out of a sixty-six million year old fossil?"

"With my own hands."

"What is it? Have you had it analyzed?"

"That's why we're here."

She held out her hand impatiently. It took him a moment to realize what she wanted. He pulled the plastic case out his pocket and dropped it in her hand.

She smiled grimly. "Then let's get to work."

KIT HAD KNOWN Arinya for years and liked her a lot. She was moody and irascible and could lose her temper at times, but she was brilliant and loved paleontology just as passionately as he did. In the lab, though, she drove him crazy. She moved with glacial slowness, checking and rechecking, unwilling to talk until she had run three different samples through a battery of tests. He wanted answers, but she didn't want to make any conclusions until she had all the information.

"These molecules are extraordinarily complex," she said, pointing at an X-ray diffraction pattern. "It looks like an

alkylpyrazine—the chemicals involved in a lot of strong odors
—but much larger. There are multiple repeating sections, too,
like a machine constructed from a set of smaller building
blocks. For instance, this section prompted it to pull in mois-
ture and reconstitute the dried chemical into a liquid when it
came into contact with the air."

"Is it really encoding a memory in its molecular structure?" Kit asked.

"It's hard to explain the phenomenon any other way, isn't
it? Not when multiple people see the same thing. I mean,
odors often have strong memory associations: you smell hot
chocolate, and you suddenly remember visiting your aunt in
the mountains as a child. The sense of smell is tightly coupled
with memory and cognitive thought. But that association is
encoded in your brain, not in the hot chocolate. It would
prompt a different memory for someone else. This seems
more like someone took a memory and imprinted it on a
molecule so it could be transmitted chemically to another individual. I don't even know how that would be possible."

"Memories have to be stored chemically in the brain,
right?"

"I don't think we have a good enough understanding of
memory to answer that definitively."

"But jump to the punchline. This actually is what it looks
like, right? A non-human species—a Cretaceous avian—had
the technology—"

"Or the biology."

"Or the biology—to communicate memories by recording
them in a physical medium that others can experience by
smelling it."

Arinya frowned. "Let's not jump too far ahead. We can't
say if this was made on purpose. It could be the result of some
surprising but natural process. Let's start with what we do
know, and then add to that knowledge through careful experi-
mentation."

"So what do we know?"

"We know this molecule prompts, in human brains, visual impressions of a scene from the Cretaceous period. The information to create the scene does not come from the human, so it must somehow be present in the molecule and be communicated through smell. Who else has smelled it besides you and me?"

"Just us. Well, with the possible exception of the fossil smuggler who found it."

"I'd like to get a larger pool of people and compare our experiences carefully. Do our brains contribute anything to what we see? Also, I'd like to try other species besides humans. Other mammals, and especially birds."

"Do birds even have a sense of smell?'

"They do," she said. "The myth that they can't smell has been around for a long time, but it's false. Many birds can locate food by smell, and some of the most intelligent species, like parrots, have a keen olfactory sense."

"But if you give a parrot a sniff of this stuff, how will you tell what it sees?"

"Well, we won't, not really. But we might be able to gauge by its reaction whether it sees something at all."

Kit rubbed at his chin. "There's one more problem."

"What?"

"There isn't any more. What I just gave you in the sample case, that's all I have."

"We'll need more if we want to answer these questions."

"We don't even know where that fossil came from. The police picked it up from a dead fossil smuggler whose partner ran off, apparently after killing him. If they could locate the partner, he might know where the fossil was found, but otherwise…"

He paused, and she noticed. "What?"

"Well, this fossil seemed to be the same species as the ones discovered by the American team I was working with. They cut and shipped out the ones they found, but it was a large site, with dozens of animals, most of which they had to leave behind. If this chemical is connected to this species, it's possible we could find more if we continued the dig."

Arinya tilted her head toward the door. "What will your escort think of that?"

"The colonel? Your guess is as good as mine."

"HOW LONG WILL IT TAKE?" the colonel asked.

Kit was starting to tire. He hadn't slept for thirty-six hours, and he had worked hard processing fossils for much of that time without very much to eat. This was a powerful man, though, one he had to please if he were to be allowed to keep working on this. "It's a large dig. I would say a few months at least." He saw the colonel's frown deepen, and rushed to explain. "As soon as we start pulling any of it out, though, people here can begin processing and studying it. We could have some more answers for you in as little as a week."

Now Arinya was frowning at him, too, probably for the implication that her entire staff would drop their current projects and work on this under the guns and scrutiny of the Royal Thai Army. He didn't think she would have a choice about that, though.

"This is the dig you worked on with the Americans?" the colonel asked.

Kit nodded. "The Americans took everything they could back with them to the United States, but there's more that they didn't have time to extract."

The colonel shook his head. "They did not take anything with them."

"Well, not exactly. They had it flown to Bangkok and put on a shipping container."

The colonel shook his head again. "They did not."

Kit remembered what the colonel had told him before, that the American team had been detained for questioning. "You mean you confiscated the fossils?" Kit felt a surge of elation at the prospect, even though he knew Samira and the others would be devastated by the loss of an entire season's worth of work.

The colonel made a gesture and said a few words to a captain, who rushed off, taking three soldiers with her. "They will return with it," he said.

A man spoke from behind them. "The substance you've found," he began, and Kit turned to see that it was Police Lieutenant Somjai. "Could it be used to force others to do what you want?"

Kit considered the question. Was he asking because it was something he wanted to do? Is that why the Army was involved? "I don't really see how," he said finally. "Smelling it does evoke a sense of terror—not just surprise at seeing the creature, but some kind of pheromone effect that directly causes fear. Someone might be able to use that to some kind of advantage over others, I suppose."

"What if that pheromone could be isolated? Into a spray, for instance, that could invoke terror in a crowd."

"Seriously?" Arinya stepped into Somjai's personal space. Even though she was a head shorter, the move made him step back. "Is that what this is about for you? Weapons development? A way to hurt people and make them do what you want?"

"Dr. Tavaranan—"

"No, you can't bully me. This isn't what my lab is for. I won't be part of some plot to control people through fear. You might tell yourself it's to keep the peace or that you'll only use it against criminals, but the truth is—"

"Dr. Tavaranan, please! You don't understand."

"What I understand is that you've practically kidnapped

me and my people and now you want us to be party to biological weapons development. If you think—"

"The weapon has already been developed!"

Arinya pulled up short. "What?"

Somjai wrung his hands, then looked at the colonel, who nodded. "The Red Wa have been coming down from the north. Selling drugs, stealing girls off the streets."

Kit and Arinya shared a look. The Red Wa were the most powerful crime syndicate in Thailand, controlling most of the country's rampant methamphetamine trade and selling thousands of young girls into sex slavery every year. They also ran most of Asia's trade in animal parts, selling elephant ivory, rhino horn, and tiger penises for use in traditional medicine. The government generally did little to stop them, since their power reached everywhere, and many policemen and politicians gladly took bribes rather than try to cross them.

"What's the connection?" Arinya asked.

"They've been offering high payments for fossils."

"That's hardly new," Kit said. "Fossil smuggling might not be as lucrative as drugs and girls, but—"

"The amounts are new," the colonel said. "They're promising more money than they could possibly get from foreign collectors, and illegal dig sites are popping up all over the province. At the same time, we're getting reports of something new on the streets. Men so intimidating that they walk into a bar and make everyone in the room wet themselves in fear. People who will then, according to the stories, do whatever the man tells them to do.

"The Red Wa have always been a problem, but they're driving other gangs out now, operating with impunity, sometimes taking over whole towns and killing the local mayors or chiefs. That's why the Army is involved."

"And you think this substance I found…"

"It might be what's giving them this power," Somjai said. "The Red Wa isn't exactly a trove of scientific research and innovation, but they certainly have chemists. If there's some way to turn a natural substance into a powerful drug, they would have the labs to accomplish it."

"I'm not going to refine it into a drug," Arinya said. "You don't need the drug in order to combat them."

"You'll do as you're told," the colonel growled.

"I won't," Arinya said. "There are some things you can force me to do, and some things you can't. Making drugs or biological weapons is over the line. You can kill me or lock me up if you want, but you can't make me use chemistry to hurt other people."

Her voice never wavered. The colonel, his face red, advanced on Arinya. "You will not speak to me this way, little girl," he said. "I will see that your family suffers for your lack of honor. You will be a shame to them, even as they suffer for your insolence."

Without thinking, Kit interposed himself between them. "Enough of that," he said, and even to his ears, his voice sounded weak and pleading. To his surprise, however, the colonel stepped back. "We'll continue the dig," Kit said. "We'll study what we find. If it comes to something more, we'll fight that battle when we come to it."

"As long as you can keep her in line," the colonel said. He spun on his heels and walked away, shoes clicking against the floor.

"So you're going to keep me in line?" Arinya asked, once Lieutenant Somjai had gone as well.

"I'd rather fight a velociraptor," Kit said, making the sign of the horns to ward off evil.

She crooked her fingernails at him and snarled.

CHAPTER NINE

66 million years ago

The air in Sharp Salt's office was redolent with competing scents: fury and fear, domination and submission, hatred and the desire to please. Prey crouched on the floor, almost forgotten except for the occasional glares directed at him by Sharp Salt as she cowered on the perch behind her desk. The roost leader, Lush Warmth of Ocean Thermals after Rain, dominated the room, not just with her scent but with her body. She was large even for a female, maybe three times Prey's body weight, and knew how to take command of a situation.

"How long were you going to keep this information from me?" Lush Warmth said, the scent suffused with rage. "You thought perhaps to solve this problem yourself? Or perhaps you thought if you ignored it, the problem would go away?"

"I...I didn't know," Sharp Salt said. Under other circumstances, Prey might have reveled in the sight of his boss groveling to a superior, but at the moment, he was too frightened by the implications of his discovery.

Suddenly, he felt the attention of Lush Warmth flooding his senses, compelling him to stand. "Child," she said, using the diminutive scent one might use to address a young boy. "Tell me what you found."

Prey carefully formed his response, expressing scent as calmly as he could, not letting emotions mix with his message. "We discovered a new orbiting body. A small one, highly elliptical, moving fast. A triumph for the program. Except..." He paused, but a rush of scent from Lush Warmth compelled him to continue. "Except that the orbit appears to be in an intercept course with the Earth."

"Appears?"

"We can't predict its path precisely enough to pinpoint the intercept. Within a hundred million strides for certain, but we can refine that the closer it gets."

"A hundred million strides."

Prey realized the number meant little to her. "The Earth is fourteen million strides wide," he said.

She snapped her jaws. "I know that."

Prey was quite sure she hadn't, but he certainly wasn't going to say so. "It will be close," he said instead. "Very close."

"But...fourteen out of a hundred," Sharp Salt complained from her perch. "That's not very likely."

Lush Warmth glared at her until she ducked her head. Then, to Prey: "When will we know?"

"We can refine our estimate as it approaches, but we won't know for sure until it strikes us or passes us by."

"And how long will that be?"

"Twenty-seven days."

Sharp Salt dropped a stink of pure terror into the air, but Lush Warmth made no reaction.

"And if it does hit, where on Earth will it strike?"

"We can't predict that," Prey said. "A small change in timing could move the impact by a million strides."

"So we don't know if it will land on our heads or the other side of the world?"

"No," Prey admitted. "But I don't think it will matter."

He explained how the debris cloud thrown into the air would block the sun for years. "I don't know if anything could survive," he said. "But I suppose our chances are better the farther away from us it strikes."

"Come with me," Lush Warmth said, and Prey stepped forward, unable to resist.

"He's mine," Sharp Salt objected. "I should come, too."

Lush Warmth struck with the speed of thought. Before Sharp Salt could react, she was prone on the floor with Lush Warmth's teeth tight around her neck. She squealed and wriggled. The scent of fresh blood flooded the air.

Lush Warmth straightened, releasing her. "Send a message to the roost leaders. We will hold a council tonight. You will stay here. Prey will come with me."

THE COUNCIL WAS HELD in a canyon shaded by a massive sequoia whose roots snarled their way through cracks in the rock. The leaders of each of the roosts gathered in comfortable nests with their advisors, rich smells of anticipation and argument filling the air. Prey had never been near so many powerful females in his life.

He stood behind Ocean Roost's nest, mostly out of sight at the edge of the canyon wall. He could pick out individual conversations from the mix of smells. Most were speculation about the reason for the summons; all of them were wrong. Beyond the canyon, guards maintained a perimeter over a mile across to ensure those same conversations were not smelled by an unauthorized eavesdropper.

Finally, Lush Warmth stood on a central, raised perch and waited for the conversation to dissipate before addressing the group. In the enclosed space of the canyon, her scent filled the air, overpowering the diminishing smells of the prior interaction. She began with formalities, praising the gathered leaders, the benefits of their peaceful cooperation, the achievements they had accomplished together. When she got to the bad news, however, she referred to it only as an important discovery and turned the perch over to Prey.

Startled, Prey stared at her, uncertain that he'd understood her. She wanted *him* to speak? He had never heard of a male addressing the Council. The assembled leaders all looked at him expectantly. He felt small and shabby. He had so often been the butt of jokes by his female roost-members that he almost expected this to be the same. Put the silly male and his crazy theories on display so we can laugh at him.

But this was no time for hesitation. The fate of the world was at stake.

Prey hopped onto the high perch, almost falling short but hooking a claw around it at the last moment. He paused for a moment, finding his balance. The august crowd waited.

He smoothed his feathers and began. He told them of the object they'd found, its size and trajectory, the efforts they had taken to refine its exact position and heading. As the scent of his message wafted through the assembly, he expressed a lighter scent containing supporting data. The leaders would ignore this, but he expected there would be astronomers among their advisors, able to process the numbers and confirm the math.

When he told them that the object would pass very close to the Earth—much closer than the moon—the audience could no longer hold back, and a rush of responding scents filled the air. Some were skeptical, wondering aloud what trick Ocean Roost was trying to pull. Others expressed only fear or amazement. Others had questions.

"There are three possibilities," Prey said, ignoring the questions for now. "The object may fly past, slingshotting around the Earth into a new orbit and continuing on its way. Even this possibility would pose a major threat: the gravitational upheaval would cause earthquakes, tidal waves, volcanic eruptions, and a deadly rain of debris from space.

"If it comes a little closer, it may be captured by the Earth and orbit us as a second moon, although one with a highly elliptical orbit. In this case, even after the initial trauma, tides and weather patterns would be radically altered, and many animals we rely on for food might not survive.

"The third and worst possibility, of course, is a direct impact. Such an event would almost certainly eliminate most life on Earth."

Argument filled the air. There was no need for speakers to wait in turn in order to express their opinions; the conflicting scents mixed and commingled, growing as each idea was received with agreement or objection, approbation or disgust. A few doubted his conclusions, but most accepted that he told the truth. Everyone seemed to have an idea about what to do, most of them involving some kind of protective building or underground shelter. None of them asked Prey for his opinion. He supposed he shouldn't have been surprised.

Lush Warmth motioned with her head for Prey to step down, but Prey wasn't ready to do that. "A shelter won't work," he said. "The effects of this collision will last for centuries. We can't just wait it out. Even a near miss would utterly change our environment. We need to adapt, not hide. We must modify ourselves to match our new environment."

An offended stink rose from the gathered females. Females didn't modify themselves. That was what one did with a tool, to shape it for a purpose. They were not tools. The idea was outrageous.

A snarl from Lush Warmth sent a shiver of fear through him, but this was too important. He kept going. "Genetic modification is the only viable approach. We need to change ourselves and our offspring to survive the new Earth."

A blast of domination silenced him, and before he could even think of resisting, he had hopped down off of the perch and abased himself on the ground. With a powerful leap that left the perch shaking, Lush Warmth took his place.

"I have already dispatched explorers to find likely caves among the ocean cliffs," she said. "You must do the same in your own territories. We have twenty-six days. If we work together, we can find shelter for all our people."

Prey dug his claws into the dirt, trying to shake off the domination. *Ocean cliffs?* Had no one heard a word he'd said? There would be tsunamis. No one along the coasts would survive.

There was nothing more he could do. When his body would obey him again, he crawled his way out from the center, ignored, and took his place against the canyon wall behind the representatives of Ocean Roost.

"Easy Prey?"

The sudden strong scent next to him made him jump. He turned to see a female and male from Desert Roost standing next to him. With the flood of strong emotions filling the canyon, he hadn't smelled them approaching.

"I am called Distant Rain Sweeping Towards Home as Night Falls," the female said. She was small, barely larger than Prey himself. He assumed on that basis that she was a low-ranking functionary. She must be smart, though, to be invited as part of her leader's retinue.

Prey faced the female and touched his head to the ground. "May your teeth be sharp and your claws strong," he said.

"This," she said, indicating the male, "is Fear Stink of Injured Mammal Limping Through the Sand."

"We think you're right," said Fear Stink. "Altering our bodies is the only way to survive this long-term."

Distant Rain bobbed in assent. "What kind of modifications do you think we need?"

Prey was shocked. He hadn't expected anyone to believe him, much less to have a female he'd never met from one of the more powerful roosts ask him what he thought.

"I don't really know," he admitted. "I would guess thicker feathers for warmth. Teeth and stomachs that can eat and digest seeds and plants instead of just meat. Maybe harder eggshells to protect our young. But I'm just making those things up. We need an expert."

"Who would be an expert at surviving a global catastrophe?" Rain asked. "It's not like anyone's done this before."

"Maybe no one. But I don't even know what can feasibly be accomplished. We need someone who knows genetics and can actually perform the changes."

Rain flicked her tail. "That's why I brought Stink. He's one of our best factory modifiers; he'll know what's possible and what's not."

Prey glanced back at the roost leaders at the center of the canyon. They circled each other, teeth bared and rear legs poised as if to spring. He doubted there would be any actual physical violence, but their body language suggested consensus was still a long way off.

"They'll be a while," Rain said. "Let's get out of here."

CHAPTER TEN

Dan Everson didn't match Samira's idea of what a CIA agent should look like. She had imagined a tall, white man, cool and composed, with clear blue eyes, strong hands, and a killer smile. Instead, Everson was short and heavy-set, with a wide, fleshy face and a receding hairline that threatened to merge with a bald spot in the back. A several-day growth of white beard contrasted with dark Mediterranean skin, roughened by the sun or maybe skin disease. He didn't look much like James Bond.

"Dr. Shannon," he said.

"Call me Samira." She shook his hand, which was warm and dry.

To her surprise, he had responded to her call by showing up in person. Less than two hours after she'd phoned, he appeared at the door of the condo she shared with Beth. She had expected to have to fight through an automated phone system and bureaucratic runaround, but Everson had seemed eager to meet with her right away. Apparently he was stationed in Colorado, not Washington. She wondered why.

Beth was out, but Samira introduced Everson to Wallace,

who sat on a perch in the living room, preening. Wallace saw him and squawked loudly enough to make Everson jump.

"He's got a voice on him," Everson said.

They sat in the living room, and Samira offered him coffee, which he accepted.

"So," he said after taking a sip. "Tell me what happened."

Samira shook her head. "First I want to understand your interest. Why did the CIA fund my research?"

He spread his fingers. "We invest in a large variety of overseas ventures. Small business startups, charitable organizations. We find that having Americans in hard-to-reach places helps us keep tabs on what's happening in the world."

It was a practiced answer, and Samira wasn't buying it. "Listen, we were forcibly detained and questioned by the Thai military, and our research was destroyed. Obviously *they* think there's something important going on. And given the speed at which you showed up here, I think you do, too."

He frowned. "Think what you like. I can't tell you what our interest in the region is. But you're right, it's more than just keeping tabs. There are important things happening in Thailand, things that affect our national security. You can help your country by telling me everything you saw and heard."

"Did you get my fossils destroyed?"

"What?"

"Was it because of your money? Did they suspect us because of you?"

Everson pursed his lips. "I'm genuinely sorry about that. But I don't think so. This goes well beyond suspicions about funding. Why don't you tell me what happened, and I'll be better able to judge?"

Samira sighed and took a long swallow of her coffee. She then repeated the story she had told Paula, focusing on the interrogation by the Thai colonel.

"This colonel, what did he look like?" Everson asked.

"Like Gandhi. In a white uniform."

"Gandhi was Indian."

"I know. Maybe it's a bad comparison. But he was thin, with a bald head and little round glasses."

Everson fished a photograph from his shirt pocket. It was a bad picture, taken from a distance and partially blocked by foliage, but Samira recognized him right away.

"Yeah, that's him."

"You're sure?"

"Absolutely. Same uniform, too, from what I can tell. Who is he?"

"Colonel Feng Zhanwei of the Strategic Support Force of the People's Liberation Army."

"Wait, the PLA? He's Chinese?"

"Born in Beijing, trained at Chengdu, an old school Maoist patriot."

So many Thais in the north part of the country had Chinese ancestry that his appearance hadn't seemed unusual. "But he was wearing a Thai Royal Army uniform."

Everson scratched his face. "Yeah, they do that sometimes. Operational security. China's influence in Thailand these days is more than most Thais realize."

"So the coup? General Wattana?"

"In China's pocket. They'll be running the place in six months. Practically are already."

"So...I don't mean to be rude," Samira said, "but why is that our business? I mean, I don't think China should be interfering with Thailand, but it's on the other side of the world. Why does the CIA care?"

Everson stared at her like she'd claimed the moon landing was a hoax. He shook his head. "I forget sometimes how little civilians know. We're at war, Dr. Shannon. Not a declared war, but a war all the same: on the oceans, in space, in the cyber security of our computer networks and financial systems and power grids. And yes, in the influence we have on other countries. China is flexing their muscles, and they're playing the game better than we are. They've got more people, better infrastructure, newer military hardware, and the will to use it. We're still ahead of them, but they're catching up fast. Our warships have regular standoffs with theirs in the South China Sea, which they claim as their national waters—not to mention Taiwan. It could flash from a cold war to a shooting war at any moment."

"And destroying my fossils had something to do with this?"

Everson slipped the picture back into his shirt pocket. "I don't know." He said it flatly, not meeting her gaze.

She rolled her eyes. "You're a terrible liar for a CIA agent. You came here with his picture in your pocket. You know who he is. Obviously you know something about his agenda."

He sat silently for a moment before responding. "How badly do you want to know?" he asked finally.

"This man destroyed three well-preserved fossils of a new maniraptoran species, the irreplaceable result of a season's work. If you know something, tell me!"

"I'm going to need you to fill out some paperwork first."

"What, like a waiver or something? Or permission for you to go through my records, investigate my background, make sure I'm a loyal US citizen?"

Everson looked uncomfortable. "We've already done all that."

"What?"

"We don't need permission to investigate you. It's all public information. The paperwork I'm talking about is a little more...invasive."

She gave him a look. "Invasive."

"Yeah. Look, if you're not interested—"

"What do you mean by 'invasive?'"

"Personal questions. About your beliefs, your lifestyle, your relationships. And you'd have to answer the same questions with a polygraph machine."

"Just so you can tell me why my fossils were destroyed?"

"More than that." He paused again, then seemed to make a decision. "Your involvement has been...requested. Insisted on, actually. By someone who can throw a lot of weight right now. Someone I personally want to keep happy. So I'm going to fast track you for a special clearance for a very sensitive program. But there are promises involved, and severe legal consequences for breaking those promises. You've got to be willing."

"Requested?" Samira was mystified. "By someone in the CIA? Who?"

"I can't reveal that. In fact, I probably shouldn't have mentioned it at all. What I need to know is, are you in? If not, I'll leave here, and you and I will never speak again."

Samira rocked back against the seat, overwhelmed. This was like Pandora's box. Should she really open a door that she couldn't close again? What if he told her about some kind of assassination plot, or about terrorist activity that could threaten people she cared about? Could she really promise to be silent about anything she was told, no matter how unethical?

On the other hand, how could she just let him walk away? She would always wonder what she could have known. It would eat her alive. She'd already lost so much potential knowledge when her fossils were taken away. How could she give up a chance to know why?

Everson watched her face expectantly. She threw up her hands. "Of course I'm in," she said. "I'm a scientist. Did you really expect me to say 'no' to learning more?"

He smiled, the first real smile he'd offered. It softened his face and made him seem younger. "Trust me, Dr. Shannon. You will absolutely not regret it."

BEFORE HE LEFT, Everson insisted she tell no one about their conversation, not about the possibility of being read in to a secret compartment, nor even about the existence of such a thing.

She showed him to the door. "Isn't this where you're supposed to say, 'I was never here?'"

"We take security very seriously," he said, the smile gone. "I suggest you start to take it seriously, too. Not a word, not a breath of implication that you have anything to hide, not even to Bethany. Lie if you have to."

The fact that he knew her sister's name startled her, but then she remembered: they'd been investigating her. Of course they knew who she lived with. "She's pretty good at noticing when I'm hiding something," Samira said.

"I'm sure you can do it. You're just upset about the fossils, that sort of thing. Improvise."

She watched him go, wondering what she had just gotten herself into and already half-regretting it.

As it turned out, Bethany had her own news and wasn't paying much attention to Samira's mood. She rushed in, her face taut with distress.

"I just got a call from Gabby," she said. "Her mother's dead."

"What? Elena?" Samira had only met her once in person, a towering figure in the field who knew more about mass extinctions than anyone else alive. She'd turned out to be as friendly and approachable a person as Samira had ever encountered, and had urged Samira and Beth to call her Elena instead of Dr. Benitez. Samira had corresponded with her occasionally for professional advice.

"What happened?"

"It was the Julian virus—that disease that's raging through Argentina. Her whole team caught it, and every one of them died. It apparently happened over a week ago, but things are such a mess down there that they didn't even get word to Gabby until today."

"That's awful."

The media had started calling it the Julian virus, since it had started in Puerto San Julian, a small harbor town in southern Argentina. From what Samira had read, there was some question as to whether it was actually a virus at all, but it was clearly infectious, and spreading fast. Over two hundred people in Argentina were dead of the disease, and a handful in other countries. To make matters worse, the virus seemed to have an unprecedented ability to cross species lines, allowing animals to spread the contagion as well. One shop owner had described a man in his store suddenly vomiting blood and convulsing on the ground, and the media couldn't stop talking about it. The CDC had issued travel warnings, and there was already talk of bans on travel to and from South America.

"Can Gabby even get home for a funeral?"

"No, that's the thing," Beth said. "She was calling to see if we could help."

"Us?"

"Well, really to see if Mom and Dad could help."

Samira and Beth's parents were experts of a sort at finding creative ways to get into countries when the straightforward approach was blocked. They had helped numerous fellow missionaries get past closed borders, and they had on multiple occasions pulled strings to help refugees gain entry to countries where they sought asylum.

Samira made a face.

"Come on," Beth said. "You know we have to go see them soon regardless. This way you'll be helping some friends out at the same time."

Samira didn't know what it said about her that she preferred the company of sixty-six million year old bones to her own parents. As Beth pointed out, though, it was unavoidable, "All right," she said. "Call them. Let's get it over with."

CHAPTER ELEVEN

Pakasit Paknikorn stopped the truck behind a warehouse in Chiang Rai. The truck had the logo of a grocery brand on the side, but he had never transported food with it. Instead, he carried heroin and meth, assault rifles, even ivory and tiger parts—whatever he was told to move. He had become one of Ukrit's lackeys, smuggling goods across the border for distribution throughout Southeast Asia. Mostly he didn't look at what they put in the truck; he didn't want to know. He just drove where they told him to drive and kept his mouth shut.

After shooting Nikorn, he knew there was no going back. The police would be after him, and even if they weren't, his sister would never forgive him for killing her husband. Better if they all thought he was dead. It was little Kwanjai he missed most of all. He had only meant to give her a better life. Now she would never leave Khai Nun, and he would never see her again.

He had fled to Tachileik, just over the border in Burma, to throw himself on Ukrit's mercy. Ukrit, it turned out, was more than just a fossil smuggler; he was a high-ranking soldier in the United Wa State Army, also known as the Red Wa. Pak had imagined Tachileik as a military encampment, but it was just a town, population fifty thousand, with a hospital, shrines, hotels, grocery stores, and clothing stores. There were even a few Westerners from Chiang Rai crossing the border to renew their visas. Beneath the placid surface, however, Tachileik was a major distribution center for drugs, weapons, and girls.

The warehouse door rolled up, and he backed the truck inside. Two men with heavy looking rifles strapped over their shoulders looked on, while other men loaded crates into the back. The man in charge spotted Pak standing nervously by the truck. "Don't just stand there," he said. "Get this stuff loaded."

Pak made a hasty *wai* and joined in the labor, lifting the crates into the bed and strapping them in place so they wouldn't slide around. He could tell they were drugs, though he didn't know what kind. He kept a watchful eye out for fossils, but they'd never been part of his cargo. What Ukrit did with the fossils that came into Tachileik was a mystery. He wasn't selling them to foreign collectors as he claimed. He was keeping them for himself. Why? Pak wasn't paid to be curious, but given his terrifying experience with the giant bird-creature on the road, he couldn't help but wonder. Did it have anything to do with how afraid everyone was of Ukrit and his henchmen? Or with the nose plugs they wore, which no one else was allowed to use? Somehow Ukrit was turning those fossils into a way to wield power over others.

Pak didn't care about Ukrit's ambition. He did want to know about the fossils, though. He couldn't bring Nikorn back to life again, but he at least wanted to understand why he had seen a giant bird that wasn't really there. There was little chance he'd find out, though. He did what he was told, anonymously sent the money he earned to his wife and sister, and thought about his daughter. He wondered what she thought of him now.

They finished loading the crates, and Pak reached for the

rope to pull down the back door. "Wait," the boss said. "We've got one more package for you."

When Pak saw what he meant, his heart sank into his stomach. One of the men led a terrified girl toward the truck, her face bruised, her hands tied in front of her with a plastic zip tie. She looked no older than fifteen.

"What is this?" Pak demanded, his pulse racing.

"What's it to you?" the boss said. "You drive the truck, that's all you need to know."

"I've never driven girls before." Pak's voice sounded weak to his ears.

One of the men carrying a rifle laughed.

"Well, then you best know this up front," the boss said. "Hands off the merchandise. She's not for you."

Pak felt his face flush. "Of course not. I would never."

"Because Ukrit would take it out of your flesh if he found out different," the boss said. "You do as you're told, you'll get your cut."

"Yes. Okay," Pak said. He couldn't bring himself to look at the girl.

One of the men led her up the ramp and used another zip tie to connect her bonds to a loop on the metal floor. They pulled the door shut and latched it, leaving her kneeling there in the dark.

Pak felt acid in his throat and tried to swallow it away. He felt sick.

"What are you waiting for, a tip?" the boss said. "Get this truck out of here."

Pak climbed into the driver's seat and started the engine. He dared not refuse. These people would think nothing of killing him. He thought of driving to the police station and turning himself in to the authorities, but the Red Wa was more powerful than the police here. They didn't let traitors live, and they would find him, even in police custody. Maybe even especially in police custody, since so many policemen were in their pay. He had no choice but to keep hauling whatever Ukrit told him to haul. That or accept that his life was over and die.

He thought of Kwanjai as he pulled out onto the highway. She wasn't much younger than the girl tied up in the back of his truck. What if it was her back there? What would he do to a man who drove Kwanjai off like a piece of meat to be sold?

Pak pounded on the steering wheel with his fist. This wasn't possible. He couldn't be this person, he just couldn't. If they killed him, they killed him. It was no more than he deserved.

He stopped the truck in an empty lot, angling it so no one driving past could see inside. When he opened the back, the girl cowered, crying.

"I'm not going to hurt you," he said. She shrieked when he pulled a knife from his pocket, but he just used it to cut her bonds.

"I'm going to help you," he said. "Get in the front."

He thought she might just run away right then, but she did what he said, climbing into the passenger seat, all the while looking at him like a mouse circling a cobra. He climbed back into the cab and started the engine.

She curled up against the door as he drove, as far away from him as possible. He thought about asking her name, but decided he really didn't want to know.

"How did you get here?" he asked instead.

She glanced at him warily, and at first he thought she wouldn't answer. Finally, she said in a tentative voice, "My father owed money. A lot of money. For drugs."

Pak's stomach twisted. He felt a surge of anger at this girl's father, but who was he to judge? He had abandoned his daughter as well.

"Do you have anyone else?" he asked. "Any other family you could go to?"

"My grandmother lives in Nong Khamin."

"Can you tell me how to get there?"

She nodded.

They drove on in silence. Was he really ready to die for this girl he'd never met? Thousands of other girls met the same fate. What difference did one make? He had no illusions about what would happen to him. He couldn't run away; there was nowhere safe. The Red Wa never forgave theft. The only thing keeping drivers from stealing the drugs they transported was the certain knowledge that they would be tracked down and killed if they did.

The thought was almost freeing. Ever since he'd shot Nikorn, he'd more or less just been waiting to die. He hadn't meant to kill Nikorn, but he'd been the one to drag him out to the hills in the middle of the night, and he'd been the one to pull the trigger. Now here he was, working for some of the worst villains in the country. What right did he have to live?

When the girl told him where to turn, he did, finally bumping the truck into a poor farmer's village. An old woman ran out of a house that was little more than a leaning sheet of corrugated metal and wrapped her arms around the girl. Pak didn't even get out. He turned and drove away, heading back to Tachileik to meet his fate.

CHAPTER TWELVE

S amira and Beth climbed into Beth's battered Mitsubishi and settled in for a two hour drive south to Colorado Springs. Samira dreaded the trip, but there was no avoiding it. They hadn't seen their parents in months, and now that they were back in the States, a visit was almost compulsory. Besides, even though Mom knew neither of them were hurt, she would be in a state of nervous apprehension until she actually laid eyes on them and could confirm with her own senses that they were safe and sound.

Route 25 took them south from Denver. While Beth drove, Samira looked out the passenger window at the Rockies, the highest ones still dusted with snow. Visiting her parents was like dancing barefoot on a floor strewn with tacks. If everyone was careful to avoid certain subjects, the visit would go smoothly. If not, then the old, unhealed hurts would tear open again, leading to fresh arguments and fresh pain. Wind buffeted the car, the flat fields of scrub grass on either side providing no barriers to diminish its strength.

A tan and red concrete sign with a stylized mountain welcomed them to Colorado Springs. A mile later, she spotted the seventeen spires of the Air Force Academy chapel off to the right, just visible in the distance. Beth took the exit, and three minutes later pulled up to a sprawling housing complex that looked like hundreds of others springing up all over the area. Mom and Dad lived here not for the Academy, but for the headquarters of Compassion International, where Mom worked as the director of sponsor services. It was one of many possible conversational landmines: Mom's job provided food, shelter, and education to thousands of children in abject poverty around the world, while Samira and Beth just dug old bones out of the ground, helping no one.

Mom and Dad stood waiting at the door for them. When Beth and Samira climbed out of the car, Mom rushed out to meet them with cries of joy, waving her hands in greeting. Dad followed behind her, only slightly more subdued. Mom was tall, with large features and a mane of frizzy hair that enveloped Samira's face as she wrapped her in a hug. Dad was almost a foot shorter, the difference emphasized by age. His beard had gone startlingly gray since she had seen him last, but his confident smile and strong hands were the same. Samira endured their kisses and overwrought exclamations of pleasure, making an effort to smile as they ushered her into the house.

The living room's eclectic, second-hand furniture didn't match, but the focus of the room wasn't on the seating. Framed pictures of children of various ethnicities decorated the walls, all of them kids that her parents sponsored person-ally: giving monthly to provide for them, writing them regular letters, and in some cases, even visiting them. Samira didn't remember the current count, but these kids had become the primary focus of their lives, with large portions of Dad's ophthalmology income devoted to supporting them.

Beth peered at a picture of an Asian girl, maybe five years old, wearing a Minnie Mouse T-shirt and standing on a dirt road. "Is this one new?" she asked.

Mom beamed and rushed to join her at the picture. "Her

name's Kwan, and she's from Thailand. Our first Thai child.
A beautiful girl. She's from the Khun Yuam district; was that
anywhere near where you were?"

Beth shook her head. "That's far to the west. Probably a
fifteen hour drive from our dig site."

"Pity."

Samira felt the first stirrings of guilt and anger in the pit
of her stomach, a feeling that would only increase the longer
they stayed. The whole practice of sponsoring children felt
crass to her, like collecting poor kids as trinkets to show off to
your friends. She knew that wasn't fair. Mom and Dad were
genuinely helping needy children, far more than most Americans even thought about. It just made Samira feel inferior and
selfish for not doing the same, and so she reacted against it.
Just sitting in this room felt like being judged and found
wanting.

"I'm worried about Camila," Mom said, moving to a new
picture, this one of a brown-skinned girl in a white dress with
red flowers. "She's from Patagonia."

"Near the Julian virus?" Beth asked.

"Not that close. But they say it's spreading."

Spreading was an understatement. The disease had raced
across Argentina like wildfire, following the lines of greatest
population. Beth told Mom about Gabby's mother and her
need to get in country, and Mom gave some suggestions and
the contact information for a local missionary as well as
someone she knew in the visa office.

"And how's little Samuel doing?" Mom asked.

Samuel was a boy from Uganda who Beth sponsored.
Mom knew all about him, of course, because it was her office
at Compassion that managed such things. They chatted about
him for a while, about how he was growing up and what he'd
said in a recent letter. No one asked Samira why she wasn't
sponsoring a child, but she felt the question hanging in the air
all the same.

"So how did it go in Thailand?" her father asked. "Find any dinosaurs?"

The knot in Samira's stomach tightened. This was landmine number two. Her parents believed that the Earth was only a few thousand years old, which made her profession a waste of time at best, and at worst, the spreading of atheist lies. "We did," she said carefully. "But the government confiscated them, so we came home with nothing."

"Oh honey, I'm sorry," Mom said.

"Was it an important find?" Dad asked. He was trying, she knew, and so she did her best to respond in kind.

"It would have been. A new species. A lot to study, a lot of published papers. Now all we have to go on is the pictures we took at the site."

The conversation stalled. It was hard to talk about details, since Dad thought dinosaurs had sailed on Noah's ark, if they even existed at all. She had tried to explain to him about radioactive dating techniques and the clarity and consistency of the history told by the rocks and fossils, but he was uninterested. The Bible was his primary source of knowledge, and anything else was secondary.

The crazy thing was, Samira understood where he was coming from. She had started at the University of Colorado as her father's daughter, as committed to Young Earth Creationism as he was now. She'd majored in biology as a road to medical school, planning to go into medical missions, just like her father. Maybe even return to Ethiopia. A chance encounter had turned that upside-down.

She'd seen a notice announcing that classes by the famed paleontologist Jack Balfour would be open for non-majors to audit. Intrigued, she signed up. In her first class, she told Balfour she was going to convince him that evolution was a myth. The result was the opposite: over the course of a semester, his careful and systematic presentation of the evidence demolished her objections one by one.

She'd begged Beth to join her, and to their parents' dismay, Beth was convinced by the evidence as well. For Samira, it was the beginning of the end: a slow eroding of everything she'd ever believed. It dismantled her faith in the Bible and in a creator God. Beth had reacted differently. She'd acknowledged the fourteen-billion-year story told by the rocks and mountains and stars and incorporated it into her faith, seeing God as the architect and orchestrator of the whole process. Samira envied her that faith sometimes, but once the edifice of her parents' belief system had been cracked, it was hard for her to accept any of it anymore.

"It was a maniraptor species," Samira said, just to say something. "That's the clade that includes modern day birds. This one lived sixty-six million years ago, right before the end of the Cretaceous. In fact, we think they might have been alive when the asteroid hit."

Mom smiled and Dad looked at something behind her head. The silence stretched.

Finally, Mom looked at Beth. "So, is Samuel into sports?"

ON THE DRIVE HOME, Beth asked, "Why do you hate them?"

Samira turned toward her, startled. "I don't," she said. Beth's face, strobed by passing headlights, was hard to decipher in the darkness.

"They're good people," Beth said. "They give to charity, they make meals for sick people, they help pull kids out of poverty. They care about you."

"I know they do. I care about them, too."

"But you sit there all evening with a scowl on your face, as if you resent just being in the same room as them."

Samira opened her mouth to deny it, but realized it was

probably true. "Maybe *I'm* not a good person. Ever think of that?"

"Don't get pissy. I'm seriously asking you. What makes you so angry?"

Samira turned toward her window and the featureless flat expanse of grass beyond it. She was angry about a lot of things. Angry that they had been forced out of Thailand. Angry that Beth could hold on to their parents' religion and love, while Samira somehow couldn't. Angry, however unfairly, that her parents had adopted her in the first place, saddling her with this ethnic, cultural, and religious mishmash that didn't fit in with any group anywhere.

She lifted a hand and let it fall. "They're just *too* good, you know? Everything feels like a judgment. Under every conversation is this subtext that I'm wasting my life."

"But you don't get that from me?" Beth asked.

"Hell, no."

Beth smirked.

"Yeah, yeah, language." Samira said. "Dad would be all over me."

"He wouldn't say anything," Beth laughed. "He'd just give you that *look*."

"Seriously, though. You know what it's like to change. To become convinced of something you never thought you'd believe. With them, there's this bright, clear line that never moves, and I'm on the wrong side of it."

"Well, you are a wicked atheist."

"Shut up," Samira said, but she was smiling.

THEY HAD ALMOST REACHED Denver when Samira said, "Doesn't it make you wonder what God's playing at?"

"What do you mean?"

"We're looking at a possible extinct intelligent species here.

Not a word about them in the Bible that I can recall. Nothing in there about *Homo erectus* or *habilis* or *neanderthalensis*, either, and now there's another sapient race, not human at all?"

"*Velociraptor sapiens*," Beth said, and grinned.

"Seriously, doesn't the narrative break down? You already have a hard time explaining how Adam and Eve could be the first humans when at least a dozen human-like species have peopled the world over the last two million years."

"And *you* have a hard time explaining how consciousness and free will can exist in a world run solely by deterministic natural laws and quantum probabilities."

A low rumble from the west. A storm coming in from the mountains. Samira reached out and gave Beth's shoulder a squeeze. That was something else bizarre about US culture that still felt wrong to her—in Ethiopia, people *touched* each other. They grasped hands and gave hugs and stroked each other's backs and arms. It communicated closeness even when words didn't.

"But doesn't this rock your belief in a good and loving God?" Samira asked. "A whole species of intelligent people, apparently wiped out? Where was God for them?"

Beth shrugged. "There are no more Assyrians or Aztecs either. Abraham and Moses aren't alive anymore. People die. We're mortal. I can't say why they died when they did, or what kind of relationship God had with them, or if they live on in heaven today. That's above my paygrade. It doesn't mean God doesn't exist, or that he's not good."

"You're always having to make excuses for God, or somehow pretend all the murder and horror is in service of some greater good."

"No, I'm not," Beth said. "There's evil everywhere; I don't deny that. The problem is, it's humans that do it. The only way to fix it would be to get rid of humanity."

Samira clenched her fists by her sides. "It's a cop out. It just means bad people can act with impunity. They can kill people and take over governments and destroy fossils and throw us out of the country, and you just sit back and say, 'It's all God's will!'"

"I don't—"

"Yes, you do. You're *nice*. You just accept things instead of fighting for them. There's evil in this world, but oh well, let's just move on, there's nothing to be done about it."

Beth's eyes flashed, and the car surged forward as she leaned on the accelerator. "That's not true or fair."

Samira pounded a fist into the dashboard and shouted in frustration. She was surprised to find that she was shaking. "All those fossils, that whole dig site: it's gone, isn't it? They're never going to let us back."

Beth took a hand from the steering wheel, found Samira's, and entwined their fingers together. "I know," she said.

From the black sky, heavy raindrops started to fall.

CHAPTER THIRTEEN

The three soldiers brought the fossils back in half a dozen oil drums. Kit looked on in horror as they emptied the shattered pieces of plaster and bone onto the preservation room floor. Had the colonel and his soldiers done this? He had almost started to believe the colonel might be a patron of sorts, a source of funding and protection for paleontology. If they were capable of this, then they were his enemies, pure and simple.

Kit and Arinya and her staff began the laborious work of sifting through the detritus, sorting and labeling and piecing together what had been torn apart. It was a jigsaw puzzle, made only slightly easier by the photographs Kit had from when the fossils were intact.

It was the start of one of the most intense and unrelenting periods of work in Kit's life, more even than writing his dissertation. These fossils represented what was possibly the most important discovery ever made, and the thought of stopping the work, even to eat or sleep, seemed unbearable. If the colonel had expected to force their cooperation, he didn't have to. He couldn't have worked them harder than they worked themselves.

Weeks went by, the two of them catching a few hours of sleep on the floor of the lab rather than finding anything better. Kit recruited several of his students at Nakhon Ratchasima Rajabhat University for field work and took them to the site to extract more of what had been left behind. They were geologists, mostly, but learned fast and worked hard, excited to be part of such a project. They didn't know the whole story, but just knowing they were digging up a new maniraptor species was exciting enough.

Kit started spending twelve-hour days on site, followed by eight- or nine-hour evenings in the lab. The whole site was situated in what would have been a deep ravine sixty-six million years ago. As the GPR images had shown, the skeletons were laid out in rows, all oriented the same way and aligned with the sides of the ravine. They recovered several skulls with an impressive array of pointed teeth, confirming that despite relatively small front claws, these creatures were pure carnivores.

Kit lived in constant fear that the colonel would tire of their lack of results and shut them down, so he moved faster than he usually would. The priority was to get the fossils out, and if a few corners were cut, that was acceptable. Better to risk losing a little information than to get none at all.

The deepest fossils were several meters down. Under most circumstances, that would be unreachable for a paleontology team, but Kit now had the resources of the Army. Once they were certain they'd extracted the upper layer, Army engineers came in and removed the intervening rock with drills and controlled explosives. Kit hovered over them, anxious to ensure that their calculations were correct and none of the precious fossils would be harmed.

He felt some pangs of guilt, knowing that if his American colleagues were here, they would be aghast at his cavalier approach. For them, good science meant taking things a millimeter at a time and recording everything along the way.

Kit felt that good science also meant taking advantage of fleeting opportunities, especially in a country where paleontology grants were practically non-existent. This was his chance. Foreign teams would eventually be allowed back, but this was the time for him to discover something important for his country, and yes, if he was honest, for himself.

Their research focused around classic questions: How had these animals lived? How had they died? The fact that the burial seemed intentional complicated matters in ways Kit wasn't prepared for. A mass grave usually meant an environmental catastrophe of some kind, a volcano eruption or earthquake or flood in which many animals died at the same time, but that wasn't necessarily the case here. Digging up a cemetery was a job for anthropologists, not paleontologists. He knew how to decipher animal behavior, not look for signs of how a civilization lived and thought.

He wasn't even sure how fossilization had occurred. The sandstone the skeletons were encased in meant they had been submerged in water, which filled the cavities in their bodies and bones, leaving sediment behind until the organic material was replaced with rock. The fact that the skeletons were still in rows suggested this had happened very slowly—a slow incursion of water rather than a flood—without disturbing the position of the bodies. But the well-preserved impressions of skin and feathers meant fossilization must have occurred very quickly, before the bodies had a chance to decay. How could both be true?

KIT DREAMED OF AN EARTHQUAKE. Maniraptors squawked in terror and ran in every direction while the world shook. In the distance, Arinya called his name. Where was she? Was she in danger?

"Kit! Wake up!"

He cracked an eyelid. Arinya leaned over him, gently shaking his shoulder. Her hair fell against his cheek. "What's wrong?" he asked, alarmed. "Are you hurt?"

"No, I'm fine. I'm great! I figured it out!"

Kit struggled to understand. He had finally gone to sleep at two in the morning after a particularly long day. "What time is it?"

"I don't know. Four or something. Who cares?" She bounced with excitement, apparently not tired at all.

Kit hauled himself into a sitting position, squinting. "What did you figure out?"

"Everything! Listen. I've been finding chemical residue of this memory liquid everywhere—on the rocks, inside the rocks, in the bones. Tiny scraps of the chemical, just detectable at the molecular level. We've been asking ourselves, what is it? How did it get spread all over?"

"And?" Kit asked. His mouth felt like it was filled with foul-tasting cotton. "You know how it happened?"

"There's only one answer that works. The whole ravine was *filled* with the stuff." She looked at him expectantly.

"Filled?" He shook his head, wondering if she wasn't making sense, or if he was just too fuzzy-headed to understand. "That would be thousands of gallons."

"Yes! And why not? We don't know how prevalent it was, how hard to produce, whether they synthesized it somehow or excreted it from their bodies or what. But listen, this explains everything! Imagine the ravine was filled with the liquid and then *sealed*, with the bodies inside. The whole area gets covered in water. Over time, the seal breaks, and water gets in, bringing sediment with it. The bodies fossilize slowly, their positions undisturbed, but preserved from decay by the liquid."

"But I don't understand. Why do it in the first place? If these creatures were able to engineer a sealed ravine filled with memory liquid, what's the purpose? Why would they dispose of their bodies in it? To provide well-preserved skeletons for future paleontologists?"

Arinya laughed. "Think, Kit! How much memory could a thousand gallons of memory liquid encode? A lifetime? A hundred lifetimes? What about the memories of an entire species?"

"You're saying…"

"I'm saying this wasn't a cemetery. Do you know what point on Earth was on the opposite side of the world from the Chicxulub crater impact site at the time it struck? Right here, where we're standing. What if that's not a coincidence?"

"You think they came here for that reason? For safety?" If so, it wouldn't have provided much. The initial shockwaves would have been dampened here compared to elsewhere on Earth, but the atmosphere would still have been filled with radioactive silt, blocking out the sun for years and killing most of the plants. Most animals living here would simply have suffered a slow death instead of a quick one.

"We already know they knew the asteroid was coming," Arinya said. "This was their solution. When these maniraptors went down into that pit, they were planning to come out again, alive. After a decade or two, once the worst of the destruction had passed, they were planning to come out again. I don't know what tech they used to survive that long, but my guess is it was pretty destructive to their memories. The memory liquid was used to preserve that. Or maybe to preserve important records for their species. This wasn't a cemetery. It was a hibernation chamber."

Kit stared at her, fully awake now. "Hibernation."

"Yeah, long-term metabolic stasis. Mammals do it, of course, but so do some frogs and lizards. A few birds can enter a similar torpor state."

"For weeks or months, not years," Kit said. "And they lose a lot of their body weight along the way."

"Maybe they had a better method. A biological ability or a better technology."

He shook his head. "That's quite a leap. If they were just hibernating, why are they all still there?"

She shrugged. "It went wrong. Maybe the devastation was greater than they imagined. Maybe whatever was supposed to cue them to wake up malfunctioned. We may never know."

KIT WAS quiet for a few minutes, considering. It did make a kind of sense, but the idea was so outlandish. "You just thought of all of this, sitting there looking at molecules in your lab?" he asked.

She blushed. "Well, I might have had a little help."

"What do you mean?"

She fished a test tube out of her lab coat pocket, unstoppered it, and held it out to him. A small amount of greenish liquid lay in the bottom.

"You're kidding. You've been sitting on this and not telling me?"

"Stop whining; I just found it a few hours ago. You were asleep."

"You could have woken me."

"I just did! Shut up and take a sniff."

Kit leaned forward warily, remembering the terror the first experience had evoked in him. He took a breath as Arinya lifted the flask to his nose. The sickly-sweet petroleum smell flooded his senses and the terror hit him, worse than before, or at least worse than he'd remembered.

Once again, the feathered maniraptor was there in the room, quick-moving and deadly, with teeth and talons meant to rend and kill. He steeled himself not to run from it, but his legs shook, and he collapsed to the floor.

A moment later, the terror vanished, as did the room. In

its place stood an open field of ferns and a clear blue sky. Fifty or sixty gray animals the size of elephants covered the field, munching on the ferns or stretching their necks to eat leaves from scattered gingko trees. Their curved backs were striped with darker bands of gray, and their long, fat tails hung in the air, balancing their bulk. Most remarkably, their heads were topped with a fleshy bulge of red skin and a bony crest, also bright red.

One of the beasts lowed magnificently and began to walk away from the clearing. Kit trotted around in front of it and bared his teeth, releasing a domination scent as he did so. The animal reared up briefly, snorting in terror, before turning and lumbering back to join its fellows. Kit circled the field, urinating briefly on clumps of plants along the way.

Another maniraptor approached, a female almost twice the size of Kit who released a domination scent of her own. Kit cowered and rested his face on the ground. She flooded his senses with another angry scent, and he turned to see that while he'd been marking territory, another of the creatures had escaped the clearing. After abasing himself once more to the female, Kit scrambled after the escaping beast.

The scene disappeared abruptly. Kit was female now, something he knew without thinking about how he knew it. He faced a pit filled with shining green liquid. The ground lurched underneath him, nearly knocking him in. The sky above was black and filled with roiling clouds. Around him, maniraptors raced in different directions, squawking, the scent of fear thick. A large wooden platform emerged from the liquid, pulled from above by ropes. As soon as it appeared, Kit scrambled aboard, followed by the others, and chose one of the nests laid out in rows on the platform. He settled into it, his heart beating wildly, as another quake shook the ravine. The nest closed around him, organic parts covering his eyes and ears. He breathed shallowly, afraid, as the platform lowered again, no time to check that everyone was in place.

The liquid covered the platform, the level rising, flowing into his nest, soaking his feathers, filling his mouth and nose. He could smell the thoughts of the others.

The vision disappeared, leaving Kit sweating and breathing hard on the laboratory floor.

"Wow," he said. "That was..." He had trouble finding words. "That was the ravine, wasn't it? And the earthquake, the clouds—the asteroid had already hit. They almost didn't make it."

"They *didn't* make it," Arinya said. "Or at least, something went wrong. They never woke up again."

He thought back. "What was that first memory then? He was a shepherd, or something like it. Keeping animals in one place while they grazed."

"I think it was unrelated. We're just getting a jumble stored in the small bits of liquid we retrieve."

Kit remembered the beasts, how large they'd been, how close and real. "Were those *Tsintaosaurus?*"

She nodded. "That's what I thought, too."

"Those have only been found in eastern China."

"Well, maybe it was a memory from China. We don't know how all these memories get captured. Or maybe *Tsintaosaurus* ranged here, too."

"They were raising them as livestock," Kit said in a voice of awe. "Animal husbandry, in the Cretaceous. How do you think they kept tyrannosaurs away from their herds?" Several Asian tyrannosaurid species had lived during that time period, and though smaller than their famous American cousin *T. rex*, Tarbosaurus and Alioramus were massive predators in their own right.

"Maybe the scent markers were enough to keep them away," Arinya said.

Kit was skeptical. "The smell of humans isn't enough to keep a fox out of a chicken coop, and the fox isn't built like a Sherman tank with teeth the size of steak knives."

"I think the scent markers we're talking about pack a little more of a punch."

Kit stood up and walked around the lab, shaking the stiffness out of his limbs. Arinya watched him, arms crossed. "What gender were you?" she asked.

"Male in the first one, female in the second. You?"

She nodded.

"Presumably I was female in the second because it was a female's memory," Kit said. "But wow, what a fascinating species. Sexual dimorphism and a clear social priority, with the females at the top."

"A female-dominated society," Arinya said. "Can you imagine?"

"It doesn't sound that great to me," Kit said.

She rolled her eyes. "Of course it doesn't. But it would be a good deal better for society and the world, that's for sure."

"Come on," Kit said. "It would be different, but it wouldn't be *better*. It would just be unfair the other way around."

She gave him a hard stare. Kit suddenly remembered that Arinya's younger sister had been deeply trapped in drug addiction and then had disappeared into the sex trafficking trade.

"I'm sorry," he said. "Your sister—I should have thought before I spoke."

"You think it's just about my sister?" Arinya asked, steel in her voice now. "I'm just sensitive because it's personal, so you can dismiss my opinion, is that what you think?"

"No. But I think an imbalance of power is bad for the weak party, no matter who it is."

Arinya advanced on him, eyes flashing. "Ever since I turned ten, my father couldn't keep his hands off of me. My mother was too afraid of him to stop it. I finally escaped to college, where my advisor told me I wouldn't graduate unless I spent more 'quality time' with him. Every step along the way, including here at the museum, I've had to fight off men who think my intellect is a joke and my body is theirs for the taking.

"Was that your experience in school? Or growing up? When you went to college, did you have to choose between staying at home in a living hell or abandoning your sister to face it alone? How often do you hear about women taking advantage of children? Or forcing themselves on their employees? It's not just because they don't have the *opportunity*. It's not at all the same, and I'm tired of obeying men because they have the power to hurt me if I say no. If women ruled the world, it might not be *fair*, but it would be a lot better than it is now."

"I'm sorry," he said. "I really am. I didn't know."

"And that's the problem, isn't it?" she said. "People only see what they want to see."

Kit didn't answer. He saw her point, but he didn't know how to say so without sounding patronizing. Finally, to change the subject, he said, "And what do you see when you look at these memories?"

Arinya shrugged. "I see people desperate to survive. They had to know their chances were small. But they banded together as a society, used their technology to create these hibernation chambers, and did the best they could."

Kit's heart raced. "You think there were more of these pits."

"There would have to be, wouldn't there, if the purpose was to save their species? The number we saw in that memory isn't enough genetic diversity to keep a species going."

"So, you think out there in the mountains…"

Her hard expression relaxed into a half smile. "There have to be more. A lot more."

CHAPTER FOURTEEN

Northeast Thailand

66 million years ago

In the end, they created thirteen pits, spread out as much as possible so they wouldn't be vulnerable to the same local effects. More would have been better, but they were limited by time and personnel. Prey, Meat, Distant Rain, and Fear Stink remained the core of the conspiracy, but there were already too many involved to truly keep it a secret. Fortunately, most of the leadership was too wrapped up in panicked infighting to take too much notice of what a few radicals—and mostly males, at that—were doing with their spare time.

Those conspirators with modification experience handled much of the difficult work, but there was still plenty for the rest to do: choosing adequate sites, sealing the pits to make them watertight, building platforms with individual nest capsules and cranes to lower them into the modification liquid. Distant Rain and Fear Stink performed the detailed molecular architecture needed to produce the liquid itself. An incredibly complex arrangement of engineered molecules that carried oxygen, regulated temperature, knitted cells, and edited genes.

"Think of it kind of like a language," Fear Stink told Prey. "There are straightforward smell-words that communicate simple things, right? A kind of food, a certain place. We combine them to create more complicated concepts, and then we combine *those* to communicate whole sentences and stories.

"Modifiers extend what we do naturally with our sense of smell into changing other organic molecules. There are simple proteins and carbohydrates and lipids and nucleic acids that we use all the time, over and over, combining them in long chains to produce new and useful properties. We keep a library of combinations, and then no one has to reinvent them for a new project, though sometimes they use them in new or creative ways. We just keep combining and combining."

"Isn't there a limit?" Prey asked.

"Not that we've found. The carbon atoms are what hold everything together, and they can be stacked together pretty much infinitely. We just snap together the types we need for the job we want to do. There are molecules to store energy, pass messages, send alerts in response to stimuli, grow new structures of different strengths or flexibility—just about anything, really, if you can figure out how. And since our bodies are made of the same stuff, we can interface directly with them, prompting them to share memories for external storage, for instance, or enter metabolic stasis."

Prey bobbed his head appreciatively. "I'm glad you're the one building it. I didn't understand half of what you just said."

"Theoretically, if we understood enough, we could create a whole individual from scratch, straight out of a modification factory," Fear Stink said. "We could even *improve* on the design, give new and useful traits or make them impervious to disease.

We can't create anything at that scale or complexity yet, but there's no technical barrier."

The idea gave Prey a chill. What could they have accomplished if this asteroid had never come? They could have rewritten their very selves to be anything they desired.

IT BECAME MORE and more difficult for Prey and the other telescope males to get away, because Lush Warmth wanted constant updates on the asteroid's position and likelihood of impact. Unfortunately, the more precise their estimations became, the greater the certainty of disaster. Even if it didn't strike the Earth, it would pass close enough to cause huge devastation. Capturing the asteroid as a second moon might even be the worst possibility, since its gravity would tear at the Earth again and again in every cycle of its elliptical orbit.

Sharp Salt took her fear and humiliation out on Prey every chance she got. She couldn't fire him from the analysis team, but she could insult and belittle him, and took every opportunity to do so. It made Prey angry, but less than it would have before. He could withstand her petty revenge, knowing that Rain and Stink and the others were relying on him. There were more important things at stake.

Every day, the asteroid grew closer, until Prey could announce with 100% certainty that it would strike the Earth. Even though they had known for weeks that disaster was unavoidable, this somehow made it seem more real. Collision. Devastation. Life as they knew it, gone. Perhaps even all life on Earth eradicated. He saw the terror he felt reflected in the faces around him.

Fourteen days until impact, then thirteen, then twelve. Prey had faced deadlines before, but nothing like this. Some couldn't stand the strain and committed suicide rather than face the doomsday. Sharp Salt reached a fever pitch of cruelty, lashing out and clawing males who got too close, until one day Crushed Neck took too long providing her a piece of data she requested, and she snapped his neck with one horrific clamp of her jaws. Some other females came and took both the body and Sharp Salt away, and Prey never saw her again.

The leadership mobilized enlargement projects for mountain caves and stocked them with fresh water and live animals for feeding. Prey knew it would be useless. The caches might possibly protect them from the initial shockwave, but the real survival challenge would be the following months and years. They couldn't stay in the caves forever. The stockpiles wouldn't last.

Prey and his friends carefully recruited more people to join them on impact day. They explained to recruits where to go and how to prepare. Recruiting too aggressively carried the risk of attracting the attention of Lush Warmth or other high leaders, but it had to be done. They had more nest capsules available than people to fill them, and Prey was determined not to leave any unused. The survival of their species depended on it.

With seven days remaining, Prey pinpointed with reasonable accuracy the location of the impact: a spot nearly on the opposite side of the world. That gave them a chance, however small. A direct impact anywhere nearby would have made irrelevant any of their plans for survival.

Five days left. The cave projects were far behind schedule, but thousands began moving into them anyway. A strict priority had been established, starting with the highest-ranking females from each roost and their choice of mate. Almost immediately, the Mountain Roost began claiming a greater percentage for their own members, since the caves were in their territory. Tensions mounted and tempers flared.

With three days left until impact, the asteroid appeared in the night sky, visible even to the unmodified eye as a bright dot little different than a star. By the following night, it was much brighter, and any secret hopes that the calculations might have been mistaken were dashed. Death was coming, and they could all see it.

On the final night, Prey sat on his perch in the empty analysis room for the last time. Nearly everyone from Ocean Roost had gone. The telescope had disbanded, but it hardly mattered; they didn't need it anymore.

He looked around at the wooden walls, the delicate organic machines, the living lungs that pumped air through the ductwork. By the next day, all of it would be gone. Even if it withstood the earthquakes and the tsunamis didn't reach this far, it would eventually rot away. A hundred years from now, there would be no trace whatsoever of the technological society that had ruled this corner of the globe. All of their accomplishments, gone.

What might they have become, if allowed to continue? Would they have filled the Earth with billions of their kind? Would they have cured disease, conquered death, visited the stars?

He hopped down from his perch. These thoughts were pointless. There was still a chance for their species to survive. As long as there was hope, he had work to do.

IMPACT DAY. The orderly retreat into the caves collapsed into chaos. The asteroid was visible now even in the daylight, a glowing orb hanging over the western mountains, prompting mass panic.

Prey and Meat worked around the outskirts, finding those too small or weak to brave the melee and telling them they had another option. They kept their distance from the narrow cave entrance, where females snarled and snapped, hurling others away to get inside. They had to be careful. If the mob at large realized that the modification pits held a chance at salvation, they would be overrun, their machinery crushed, their hard work demolished. At the same time, they still had empty nests, and the more they could save, the better the chance for their species as a whole.

The asteroid flared suddenly bright as it reached the atmosphere and then disappeared over the horizon. They watched it for a moment, shocked into stillness, and then everyone ran for the cave at once. Growls and screams rang out, and the air filled with the stink of blood and terror. Prey watched in horror, unable to tear away.

Meat tugged at him. "No more time. Let's go, right now!"

Prey turned his back, knowing that everyone he was leaving behind would die. Why couldn't he have saved more? He should have worked harder to convince the leaders, to make them listen. They could have done so much more if they had all worked together!

He increased his strides, bounding after Meat, but paused when he smelled more blood and heard a whimper from a ditch. He stopped and looked down. Distinguished leader Lush Warmth of Ocean Thermals after Rain lay prone, blood staining her feathers.

"What are you doing here?" Prey asked.

Lush Warmth's reply was weak, barely detectable above the sharp scent of her blood. "Tried...to keep order. Make them stay in line."

"And they attacked you?"

Meat reappeared at his side. "Leave her! There's no time."

Prey knew he was right, but something snapped in his mind. He wasn't going to leave one more behind if he could help it, no matter who it was. He climbed over Lush Warmth and took up a position on one side of her body. "Help me!"

"We can't lift her," Meat objected. "She's too heavy. We'll never make it. She'll never survive anyway."

"I'm not going without her."

Meat growled, but he took the other side. Together, they

heaved her to her feet. She couldn't walk on her own, but she could partially support her weight. They stumbled toward the modification pits as the asteroid fell toward the planet.

They didn't make it.

THE FLAMING ball fell unseen behind the horizon. For a time, there was nothing, as if it had simply ceased to exist. Then the shockwave hit.

The ground bucked like an angry beast, and a sound like all the trees in the world breaking ripped through the clearing. Prey, Meat, and Lush Warmth were tossed into the air like stones, only to crash to the ground again a dozen strides away. Wind screamed past, tearing at their feathers, whipping away any smell. Prey felt dazed and blind, stunned by the power of it. They were on the opposite side of the world! What must it have been like closer to the impact?

They helped Lush Warmth up again and staggered on. The wind now brought the reek of smoke with it. Dirt and debris whipped against their faces. The earth heaved again, knocking them off their feet. Prey knew that would keep happening, like ripples in a pond. The air was already growing unbearably hot. That would continue, too, as the searing heat from the impact expanded around the world toward them. Lethally hot, and then, once the heat dissipated, lethally cold.

They pressed on and finally reached the nearest modification pit, where they found another scene of chaos. Wooden cranes stood along the edge of the pit, holding cages to lower them down, but half of them had fallen. Males and females alike fought each other for the remaining positions.

The pit was still filled with the dark liquid, fortunately not broken open by the earthquakes. If the liquid had run out, they would all have been doomed. The cranes were meant to lower open cages into the liquid. Each wooden cage contained six nests. All the operational cranes were already in use, with their nests full and others fighting to be next.

Prey felt like his skin was on fire. He looked up into the sky, which was already darkening with swirling dust and ash. This was the end.

There was no way to communicate through scent. The wind whipped away their own smells, which were dominated anyway by the burning reek. "Over here!" Meat verbalized in the low-caste male language, as loudly as he could over the roar of the wind. A still-standing crane held a cage of empty nests. The fact that no one was fighting over it meant something was wrong, but perhaps they could fix it.

Prey examined it quickly and realized that the friction winch, designed to lower them gently without intervention once the nests were filled and closed, had jammed. He could break it, but then the cage would simply fall into the liquid without him on board.

"Go!" Lush Warmth called, surprising Prey by using the males' verbal language. "I'll release it once you're in place."

"But you'll die!" Prey said.

The distinguished leader bobbed her head sadly. "Even if I were to make it through, I would not survive. We should have listened to you. Go, and live for all of us."

Prey didn't wait to be asked twice. He and Meat scrambled up to the hanging cage. They slipped into capsules and sealed themselves in. As the next quake rumbled under their feet, Lush Warmth wrenched the winch free, and they fell with a splash into the liquid below.

Prey panicked as he sank, the cold liquid soaking his feathers. The world above him was dying. How could he possibly think this hastily-constructed effort would be able to save them? Instead of his salvation, this could very well be his tomb.

He willed himself to relax. The liquid that now reached his neck was the most sophisticated technology his people had ever invented. He trusted Fear Stink and Distant Rain, and all the others who had devoted the best of their minds and labors to this project since the asteroid had been discovered. There was nothing left to do but let it run its course, for good or for ill.

Prey gave himself over to the liquid, letting it fill his mouth, and slipped away into darkness.

CHAPTER FIFTEEN

The deeper Kit and his students dug at the site, the more green liquid he and Arinya were able to extract back at Sirindhorn. Sometimes smelling it would prompt long sequences of visions; sometimes it would prompt none at all. Each vision began with the image of a single maniraptor, and they theorized that each was tagged by the raptor whose memory it belonged to. They began to catalog the visions they experienced, trying to put together a fuller picture of their civilization and what had happened to it.

The maniraptor society was dominated by the females and marked by dramatic sexual dimorphism, with the females substantially larger than the males. It was also a technological society, though their technology didn't look like anything human. The maniraptors hadn't learned how to work metals or harness electricity, but their ability to manipulate organic chemistry and genetics far surpassed anything humans could do. They created machines out of living creatures, fueling their industries with plant matter rather than fossil fuels. Their primary communication was chemical, through their sense of smell, which allowed them to share detailed and precise data.

They even had a form of computing, using individuals as nodes in a network.

Kit finally figured out that the maniraptors standing in a hexagonal pattern on the hill in the first vision he saw was a form of telescope. They were performing astronomical inter-ferometry, communicating the sky views from each male as scent data and combining it mathematically into a single, high-magnification image. Humans did the same thing with multiple telescopes to simulate an aperture larger than what could actually be built with a lens. It took computers and complicated mathematics to make it work. The maniraptors seemed to be able to do it simply by combining their mental efforts and scent data, using the eyes and brains of a hundred individuals working together.

"They actually changed the focal length by tightening the pattern of where they were standing," Arinya said. They were both beyond exhausted, but giddy with the excitement of discovery upon discovery. They could almost forget they were being forced into it by men with guns. Almost.

Finally, the painstaking work at the dig site started to uncover the next maniraptor of the twenty-seven skeletons discovered by Samira's ground-penetrating radar. The bones were encrusted with a hardened layer of the green liquid and the skeleton, actually faintly visible through the translucent material, seemed incredibly well-preserved. It would take a month to pull it out with the care it deserved, but Kit knew they couldn't rely on having that much time. The colonel wasn't a patient man.

Kit and Arinya spent every moment working. Even when they stopped to eat, they talked about what they were learning and had yet to learn. Arinya had even managed to identify which part of the giant organic molecule delivered the initial image of a maniraptor and which comprised the rest of the message.

"How is it that it works for us at all?" Kit asked. "How can memory liquid meant for ancient maniraptor brains have the same effect on ours?"

Arinya lifted an arm behind her head and pulled on it with the other hand, stretching tight muscles. "We test psychiatric drugs on animals all the time. Mostly mammals, of course, but if drugs to treat human depression or psychosis can be adequately tested on rats, it seems reasonable that hallucinogens that worked on ancient birds might work on us, too."

Kit thought about that. "Maybe scent communication is more universal than voice communication," he said. "It's more fundamental to animal behavior patterns, and it directly affects neurochemistry. It's tied to emotion, social hierarchy, and memory in thousands of species, through direct chemical experience. Voice communication doesn't come close."

"For many animals, it's their primary sense," she agreed.

"Do you think this is what the Red Wa have been using to control people?" Kit asked.

She took a step closer, looking at him oddly. It made him feel nervous.

"Arinya?"

She didn't say anything, just took another step with that same expression, as if she were waiting for him to react. His sense of anxiety increased.

When one more step caused a brief surge of fear, he figured it out. "Wait. Are you wearing...?"

"How do you like my new perfume?" she asked, grinning.

"You put some of it on yourself?"

"Just a tiny sample on my shirt collar," she said. "I wanted to see what the effect would be on you." She raised her voice. "Now bow down and worship me!"

Kit just looked at her. "Um..."

She looked disappointed. "Maybe I didn't put enough on."

"If I can smell it, why am I not seeing a vision?" Kit asked.

She gave him a smug smile. "I isolated the key molecule and extracted it. Terror and dominance, but no vision."

"Seriously? But that's what the colonel wants, isn't it? That's what the Red Wa are using. Are you going to tell him?"

"Well, it doesn't seem to work. Let me try again." She handed him an empty test tube. "Drop that," she said.

"No."

She tried again more imperiously: "Drop that right now!"

He shook his head. "Nope. I don't even want to a little bit."

She retreated to one of the lab tables, where she'd organized rows of spray bottles. "I've sorted them by strength. The one I used was a pretty low-hierarchy individual, and I didn't use very much. Maybe if I—"

"Wait," Kit said. "You think these memories communicate hierarchy as well?"

"They aren't just memories." Arinya fiddled with the sample cases while she talked. "This is how they communicated. I think their whole civilization revolved around this stuff. It doesn't just capture a memory in chemical form. It expresses the will of the individual doing the communicating."

Kit sat down on a lab stool. He wasn't getting enough sleep. "Sorry, you're losing me."

"Lots of animals have pecking orders," she said. "Birds certainly do—hence the name. Most mammals have social hierarchies, with an alpha male getting first shot at food and sex. Those at the top exert their will on the others. How do they do it? Some of it is through fighting and fierce display, but a lot of it is through smell. Most animals have scent glands they can use to mark territory, claim females or offspring as their own, or warn off a rival.

"These maniraptors took it a step further. We already know they communicated primarily through scent, not voice, right? That bit at the beginning where you see an image of the maniraptor—I think it's more than just identification. I think it's that individual expressing dominance—establishing their rank, if you will. It's why it universally evokes terror in us. They all rank higher than we do. To a maniraptor, however, whose whole social standing is based on who can dominate whom, it tells you who they are and how important they are in society.

"In person, of course, they could just exude scent. Across distance and generations, though, scent doesn't last. I think they also use these chemicals like a written language. These aren't just memories. They're recordings of the scent chemicals they used to speak to each other. That's why they put so much of it in their hibernation chambers. It's their library."

KIT COULDN'T SLEEP that night. He had lied to Arinya. The truth was, he *had* wanted to drop the test tube. It had taken all his willpower to keep his grip. She had used a tiny sample of a low-ranking individual, and it had nearly dismantled his will entirely.

It was a horrible feeling. As if a switch had flipped in his brain, slaving his will to hers. Holding on to the test tube had seemed almost unimaginable, like something he could wish for but never achieve. It might have been muscle reflex more than anything else that had given him the power to hang on. If she had tried again, it would have fallen for certain.

He'd successfully distracted her from a second attempt, but he doubted he could hold her off for long. And then what? If they told the colonel, he would force them to give him the secret, and then he would have the same power.

As much as he wanted to support the Thai military, Kit wasn't sure he trusted the colonel that far. There had been signs that he might not be everything he claimed to be. Snide comments about the Thai royalty, inappropriate for a high-ranking Thai officer. A phone call conducted in Mandarin. If the Red Wa had this power, he supposed it made sense for his government to have it too. But he didn't want to hand it over to the Chinese.

He needed help. Someone he could trust to be loyal to Thailand, with contacts and influence at the highest level.

On the wall of the laboratory were two photographs, side by side. The first was a black-and-white shot of the older Princess Sirindhorn, the woman the museum had been named after. The second was of the younger Princess Sirindhorn, speaking at a microphone, her impassioned expression urging her listeners to action. The princess's fiery condemnation of police corruption, drugs, mistreatment of the hill tribes, and especially the selling of young women as sex workers, was legendary. The royal family in Thailand was barred from participating in politics—Princess Ubolratana had caused a huge backlash years before when she tried to put her name in as a candidate for prime minister—but Sirindhorn had found a middle ground as an activist.

And just like that, Kit knew who to ask for help.

Arinya snored gently in her cot across the room. Kit climbed carefully to his feet and collected the vial he needed. The soldiers were accustomed to him leaving early in the morning to go to the dig site, and given his willingness and obsessive work habits, no longer accompanied him. This time, however, he had another destination in mind.

He navigated the parking lot by moonlight and made his way to the pickup truck he used to get to and from the site. It was one of the same two trucks he had acquired for the American team to use, and contained a lot of the same equipment. He eased behind the driver's seat, his heart pounding. So far, he wasn't doing anything he hadn't done on other mornings, but he felt terrified of being caught anyway.

He shut the door and started the truck. A sharp rap on the

window right next to his ear caused him to jump and bleat in surprise. Arinya peered at him through the window. Trying to still his breathing, he lowered the window.

"What are you doing?" she demanded. "I saw you take that vial. Where are you going?"

He sighed. "You might as well climb in."

HE EXPLAINED ON THE WAY. "She's rich, she has all kinds of contacts in government, and she's passionate about human rights. Even better, she's not part of the government herself, and she's absolutely loyal to Thailand. If anybody can help, she can."

"But why didn't you tell me?" Arinya asked. "I've been suspicious of the colonel from the beginning. I don't want to give him power over any kind of weapon, much less one that might let him control people. Why would you leave me out?"

Kit blushed. "I...well, it's dangerous. If the colonel found out and threw me in jail, I might never see daylight again. I didn't want to endanger you as well."

Arinya gave him a look. "Chivalry is dead for good reason," she said. "Don't treat me like a child. Tell me and let me make my own choices."

According to Princess Sirindhorn's published speaking schedule, she was in the middle of a three-day conference in the town of Kalasin. Kit had no idea how hard it would normally be to get an audience—quite difficult, probably—but this was an emergency. He had a secret weapon in his pocket, and he was prepared to use it. They arrived just as the sun rose in the eastern sky.

Before leaving the truck, Kit unstoppered the vial and applied a small amount to his shirt collar. A sickly sweet smell filled the small space.

"I can't believe you lied to me about that," she said.

"I'm sorry," he said, handing the vial over to her.

"Wait," she said. "You haven't even tested it. Tell me to do something."

"Okay. Pull your hair."

Immediately, she yanked on her hair. "Ow!" she said, but she kept on pulling it viciously.

"Stop!" Kit said, horrified.

She dropped her hands, breathing hard. "Well," she said. "It works."

AFTER THAT, it was surprisingly easy to see the princess. Kit was careful not to make any commands, just gentle suggestions, and that was more than enough. The speed and eagerness with which people responded disturbed him. Was he doing the right thing, to manipulate them in this way?

"Don't worry about it," Arinya said. "They *should* let us in to see her. In order to convince them, though, we'd have to show them what we've got, and we don't want too many people knowing about it. This is the best way."

Finally, they were led to a hotel room where a black-suited man opened the door and let them in. A petite young woman in an expensive suit sat in front of a mirror, applying lipstick. She turned in surprise as they entered.

"Mongkut," she demanded of the black-suited man. "Who is this?"

"They needed to see you, your majesty," he said.

"So you just let them in? Without consulting me?"

Kit gave the deepest *wai* he could manage, nearly touching his head to the ground. "Your majesty, forgive us. We didn't know who else to turn to."

Her expression cleared. "Of course, it's no problem," she said.

Kit didn't want to force her compliance. He wanted her

willing help, and he wanted that help to continue after he left the room. "Do you have any cotton balls?"

The princess gave him a strange look, but she indicated her makeup kit. "I do."

"I'm sorry," Kit said, "but please put them in your nose."

Princess Sirindhorn did so without complaint. A few moments passed, and then she stood and backed away from them. "What is this? Who are you?"

"We don't want to hurt you," Kit began, and then stopped, realizing that this was exactly what a kidnapper or terrorist might say.

Arinya came to his rescue. "We have solid information on how the Red Wa are gaining power and forcing women to do their will. We're afraid the Thai military is using similar tactics, and we think the Chinese might be involved."

Princess Sirindhorn sat on the bed. Kit had seen her on television projecting a commanding presence and calling men in power to account. Now she just looked young and small.

"How did you do that to me?" she asked.

Kit explained. He told her about the substance found in the fossil dig, about its ability to inspire fear and obedience, and about the colonel and his soldiers.

"And this chemical. It can make people do anything?"

"I don't know the limits. We only just discovered it, and we haven't told the colonel yet."

"Mongkut," the princess said sharply. The black-suited man appeared again. "This man is going to tell you to do something. Under no circumstances are you to do it. Do you understand?"

Mongkut looked confused, but he nodded.

Kit looked at him, thinking. "Take your shoes off."

Mongkut looked at the princess in alarm, but he obediently removed his shoes. "I'm sorry, your majesty," he said. "I just"—his expression grew more tortured—"I just couldn't help it."

"Give your shoes to me," Kit said, and Mongkut obeyed, though he growled and apologized to the princess as he did.

"All right, that's enough," she said.

Kit gave him his shoes back. Princess Sirindhorn told him not to worry about it and returned him to his post.

"You could have asked for his gun instead of his shoes," she said. "You could have killed me, or maybe even made him do it."

Kit nodded solemnly. "That's why we need your help. We don't want this to be in the wrong hands. Or really, in any hands. We don't know what to do."

The princess stood, and the look of passionate command returned to her small frame. "You did the right thing," she said. "This needs to be used as a force for good, not for evil."

"I'm not sure it should be used as a force for anything," Kit said.

"And yet you used it today. To come see me."

"That was because..." He stopped. Of course she was right.

"Because it was good," the princess said. "Because it needed to be done. Listen, hundreds of young women and girls are forced into sexual slavery in Thailand every year. Many stay in the country, attracting millions of foreign tourists. Hundreds more are exported as slaves to men in other countries. Is that what you want our proud nation to be known for? The rape and mistreatment of our own young girls?"

"No," Kit said, "Of course not."

"And if you had the power to rescue these girls, and did nothing, what would that make you?"

He didn't know what to say to that.

Arinya answered instead. "You're right," she said. "Nobody does anything, because nobody thinks they can."

The ferocity in her voice caught the princess's attention. "Someone close to you?" she asked.

"My sister," Arinya said. "She got caught up in drugs. We tried to help her, but we couldn't, and then one day she was gone."

"I'm sorry. It's the story of so many. You said the supply of this chemical is at Sirindhorn Museum?"

"Yes," Arinya said. "And we can extract more, now that we know how to do it."

Kit looked between the two women. "Wait, extract more?" he said. "I don't think—"

The princess put a hand on Kit's shoulder. "You did well, coming to me. Now trust me."

He bowed again into a deep *wai*. "Your majesty."

"My friends call me Mai."

Kit felt his face burning. Most Thais had personal nicknames, usually short and cute names given at birth like Nok, Pet, Lek, or Uan. They meant things like 'bird' or 'duck' or 'tiny' or 'fat,' and were used by family and friends throughout life. Mai meant 'new,' and the idea that a royal princess had just invited him to use her personal name, like a close friend, left him floored.

"Mai," he said tentatively. "I do trust you. You are welcome to everything we have."

"Do you have more of the chemical you can leave with me right now?"

Kit didn't hesitate. He had come here for help because he didn't know what to do, and she seemed to know exactly what to do. He pulled the vial out of his pocket and handed it to her.

"Thank you," she said. "Go back to the museum. Tell no one what you've found or that you've spoken to me." She gave them her personal cell phone number, which made Kit blush all over again. "I will investigate who this colonel is, and then I will come to you."

"Come soon," Arinya said.

CHAPTER SIXTEEN

S amira met Dan Everson at a grubby diner with a gravel parking lot and a broken neon sign. She climbed into his pickup, and he pulled out without a word, turning west. They drove for nearly an hour, weaving through cuts in the mountains, sometimes heading north, sometimes west again, the roads getting smaller, until Samira had no idea where she was. Finally, he turned off the road altogether, following what seemed to be little more than a dirt path through a rocky valley.

It occurred to her that she was being driven out into the wilderness by a man she didn't know, with only his word for it that they were headed for a super-secret CIA facility where they would reveal wonders to her. In fact, now that she thought of it that way, it seemed pretty ridiculous. Was she that gullible? She had, at his instruction, specifically told no one where she was going. She glanced at him and then back out at the empty canyon. She was a fool. Any moment now, he was going to stop the car and pull a gun on her.

Surreptitiously, she slipped her phone out of her pocket and checked it. No service. Of course not. In the stories about stupid girls who drove out into the middle of nowhere with psychopaths, there was never any cell phone service.

"That won't work out here," Everson said. "In fact, you're not allowed to take it into the facility. Might as well put it in the glove compartment."

She put it on the seat next to her instead, so she could keep checking. Was this going to be her story? The naive young woman who follows the villain into the desert and is never heard from again? They would never find her out here. Her body would be left to rot and be eaten by vultures.

Was there really a secret CIA facility? The paperwork had seemed real enough. Would a psychopath really go to all the trouble of creating fake CIA paperwork? She wished she'd at least told Beth, despite his clear instructions to the contrary.

A friend who lived alone once said that whenever she felt scared that someone might break into her house and kidnap or murder her, she had a foolproof strategy: she would walk like an Egyptian and shout "Moldy potatoes!" Because the victims in those kinds of stories never did anything like that. So the fact that she was doing it meant she couldn't be in that kind of story.

Samira smiled at the memory and whispered "Moldy potatoes!"

"What?" Everson asked.

"Nothing. I just...how long until we get there?"

"Not long now."

EVENTUALLY THEY REACHED a serious-looking fence and a gate. The pair of guards manning it wore full-helmet gas masks and carried assault rifles. They scrutinized Everson's ID and asked for her drivers license. One of them took it away with him and spoke on his radio for what seemed like a long time while the other watched. Finally, they returned her ID and waved them through.

A large sign on the fence caught her attention.

RESTRICTED AREA WARNING

This area has been restricted by authority of the installation commander. All persons herein are liable to search. Photography of the facilities is prohibited. Unauthorized entry is prohibited. Deadly force is authorized.

DESPITE THIS DIRE WARNING, the fence seemed to be guarding nothing. The same rocky soil and sparse shrubs appeared on both sides, with no buildings, weapons, or alien spacecraft in sight. They drove on for several more minutes before a squat tan building appeared on the far side of a small rise. The building was small, barely large enough to house a daycare, but it had a solid look, like it might survive a bombing strike. Fifty yards away from the building, at the end of a track, stood a white geodesic sphere that Samira guessed housed a satellite dish.

"What is this place?" she asked.

"You're about to see."

A door opened and he drove inside, down a ramp that led to an underground parking garage. A surprising number of cars filled the space, given the size of the building above.

"Why build a garage?" she asked. "You've got plenty of room for parking on the surface."

"Counter-surveillance," Everson said. "The larger the parking lot, the bigger the facility. From space, this just looks like a minor installation."

"And it isn't?"

Everson didn't answer, but a smile played at the corners of his mouth.

They parked and walked to an elevator, their footsteps echoing against the concrete walls. Everson waved a badge and typed numbers into a keypad. The doors slid open, and they stepped inside. The numbers on the elevator buttons were reversed and ran from "1" at the top of the panel down to "8" at the bottom. A display above the door showed the number "1" in red.

"There are eight underground levels?" she asked.

"Twelve, actually," Everson said. "But you need another elevator to get down to the lower floors. There's a freight elevator, too, that goes up to the surface and services all the floors. We couldn't do what we do here without that."

The elevator jerked and started to descend. When the doors opened again on the eighth floor, Samira got yet another surprise. The place was enormous, with a high ceiling like a warehouse. It covered much more area than either the squat building above or the parking garage. She saw laboratory areas and plastic-enclosed clean rooms, computer displays and, to her astonishment, fossil treatment tables and equipment.

"It's like Cheyenne Mountain," she said.

"Sort of. Except everyone knows about NORAD, and nobody knows about this. Plus, NORAD was built to survive a nuclear explosion, with huge blast doors and radiation filters and giant springs to withstand impact and all that. This is more like a big cave. If we got hit by a nuke, we would all just get buried by tons of rock."

"Comforting," Samira said.

"Not to worry. Nobody's going to bomb us, because they don't know we're here."

They walked through the room. The dozens of people working there took little notice of them. The fossil preparation tables looked like those at any university or museum facility, with lights and microscopes, air compressors and pneumatic tools, needles and vises. Plaster shells lay propped up against table legs, and stone detritus littered the tabletops.

As they passed, a man in a white lab coat took a drill with a thin bit, maybe a sixteenth of an inch, and held it to the side of an otherwise pristine pelvic bone.

"Hey wait, what are you doing?" Samira said, but the man activated the drill, driving a neat hole into the bone. He turned it off when he saw her and pulled off the protective goggles he'd been wearing.

"Samira?"

She took in his thick mustache, large nose, high forehead, and graying hair. "Professor Rivero?"

He clasped her hand, then pulled her in for a hug. "So they brought you in, too. I'm glad."

"Professor, what—"

"Please, you can call me Matias now."

"Aren't you still teaching at the university?"

"Oh, a few hours," he said. "I'd like to do more, but you know." He raised both hands, indicating the activity around him. "It's hard to say no to this."

"But why are you drilling that fossil?"

"Least invasive method," he said. "You let the agency boys at it, they would just pulverize it and boil out what they need."

"Pulverize?" she repeated, horrified. "Why? To boil out what?"

Rivero traded glances with Everson and gave Samira a sheepish smile. "You're new, I guess?"

"First time down the elevator," Everson said.

"Well, I'll let you get on with the tour, then. It's a lot to take in at first, but you were always a quick student. It'll be great to have you on the team!"

Samira opened her mouth to ask more, but Rivero had already turned back to his table, and Everson was hustling her along.

"What's going on here?"

"All in good time," Everson said. "Suffice it to say, this is where much of the preparation, extraction, and testing is done. Above us is mostly office space: computer analysis, administration, that sort of thing. We have a few more floors to visit, though."

This time, the elevator was red and painted with the words "AUTHORIZED ENTRY ONLY." Everson waved his badge at a reader, and the doors opened.

Inside, there were buttons for floors eight through twelve, and Everson pushed the eleven.

As the doors slid shut, Samira said, "Aren't you going to tell me what all of this is for? It's not much of a tour if I don't know what I'm looking at."

"Five years ago, a farmer in northern Thailand stumbled on something remarkable."

"What was it?"

"We don't know. We never saw it. Well, by now we have a pretty good guess what he found, but at the time we had no idea. All we knew was that China came down on it hard. They mobilized their Ministry of State Security in hours and then took over. Anything that was found there, they whisked it away and kept the knowledge pretty closely held. None of our contacts had any idea what they had."

The elevator doors slid open on a hallway, and Everson stepped out, still talking. "Since then, we've been all over the Thai paleontology scene, and so have the Chinese. Black market prices are ten times what they were five years ago, but China keeps paying, and we do, too."

She followed him down the hallway, aghast. "You're buying black market fossils?"

"Got to. Or they all just go to China, and we don't get a thing. Don't worry, we're treating them well. We've got top-tier scientists in here; you just saw one of them."

"But smugglers aren't scientists. They damage the fossils

they take as often as not. And the bones are only half the story; without knowing where they came from, without studying the surrounding rock layers, you lose most of the information."

Everson shrugged. "If I could put you on the ground in Thailand with twenty of your peers and let you do your thing, I'd be a happy man. But it's not our country, and China's got twice the influence there that we have."

"You think my fossils ended up in China?"

Everson looked thoughtful. "There's a good chance of that," he said. "But most of the Chinese action on this is coming from their version of CIA, the Ministry of State Security. Colonel Zhanwei's with a different crowd; he's military, ex-Special Forces before joining the Strategic Support branch. The MSS has been working through the organized crime element, whereas Zhanwei's working through the Thai army. So there's a chance he represents a competing interest."

He led her into a conference room where two people were already seated: an Asian woman dressed in a dark business suit and a soldier in fatigues. "Samira, meet my assistant, Michelle Jiankui. And this is Captain Hugo Gutierrez, United States Army."

Samira nodded at them nervously.

"Have a seat, please," Everson said.

Samira took the chair opposite Michelle. Everson sat at the head of the table.

"Captain Gutierrez here is the detachment commander for a special forces unit that specializes in mountain combat and hostage extraction. He and his team are preparing for a mission to the Kalasin province in northern Thailand."

Samira looked at Gutierrez and then back at Everson. "Hostage extraction? Who's the hostage?"

"In this case? A very valuable theropod dinosaur."

CHAPTER SEVENTEEN

E verson explained the situation.

"One of the geology students at Nakhon Ratchasima Rajabhat University has a gambling problem. We've been helping him out with his debt, and in return, he's been reporting to us on what's happening there at your old dig site."

"One of Kit's students?" Samira asked. "I mean, Professor Kittipoom Chongsuttanamanee?"

"Yes, Professor Chongsut..." Everson cleared his throat. "Kit, as you call him, is working for Colonel Zhanwei now. They have continued excavating the site and have discovered an extraordinarily well-preserved specimen."

"Kit wouldn't work for that bastard," Samira said, though in truth she wasn't sure. Given a choice between working the site and not working it, he might take any benefactor he could get. She might, too.

"He may not know Zhanwei is Chinese, or he may not have been given a choice," Everson said. "Whatever the reason, he is most definitely working for Zhanwei. We need to act before they remove that fossil from the ground."

Samira rubbed the back of her neck. "I'm not getting

this," she said. "You want this fossil simply because the Chinese want it? If they started collecting seashells from the beach, would you want those, too?"

"There's a bit more to it than that."

"Exactly. There's something you're not telling me. You talk about a well-preserved fossil, but from what I can see upstairs, you're just smashing them. Clearly you're not in this to expand our understanding of Cretaceous morphology. What are they extracting up there on the eighth floor? What is this really about?"

"All in good time, Dr. Shannon," Everson said. "We operate under a strict need-to-know basis here. The more you can contribute to our efforts, the more you'll be trusted with the details. I can assure you, though, we want this fossil intact."

"You want my help without telling me what it's for?"

Captain Gutierrez huffed a tiny laugh and spoke up for the first time. "Welcome to the military."

Samira pushed her chair back. "I'm sure you're used to running off to foreign countries and killing people because somebody told you to," she said. The smile on the captain's face disappeared. "But I prefer to know why I'm doing something before I do it."

"Now, listen," Gutierrez began, his face turning red, but Everson held up a hand, and the captain closed his mouth.

"Dr. Shannon, if you want explanations before you act, perhaps you could refrain from insulting people before you know them."

Samira winced. "You're right." She met Gutierrez's unfriendly gaze. "That was out of line. I'm sorry."

"No problem," Gutierrez said, though his expression didn't get any friendlier.

"This is the deal," Everson said. "Captain Gutierrez is flying a mission to Thailand. His team leaves tomorrow. He needs to know everything you know about that site. Its exact location, the surrounding terrain, nearby roads, everything. Then he needs to know how to pull it out of the ground in less than an hour without breaking anything."

Samira gave an incredulous laugh. "In less than an hour? Without breaking anything? It's embedded in rock."

"Without breaking anything important. They will use precision explosives to—"

"No. No, no, no."

"What's the problem, Dr. Shannon?"

"This is insane. It would take months to excavate even one complete fossil from that site without damaging it. There are twenty-seven skeletons down there, and there's no possible way to remove one with *explosives* without irreparable damage, probably to all of them. A proper scientific survey takes—"

"This is no scientific survey," Everson said.

"That much is obvious."

"This fossil is of paramount importance to national security," Everson said, his voice rising. "We are going in, and we are taking it out. You can help us to do it better, or you can go home."

She stared at him. "How can a sixty-six million year old dinosaur possibly be critical to national security?"

"You don't really need to know that."

"You want me to help you get it home without damage. But you clearly don't care about the kind of damage I care about. How can I help you if I don't even know what you're trying to preserve? When you recruited me, you led me to believe you would be explaining things to me. You want my help? Explain."

The room fell silent. She held Everson's gaze, though she was already doubting herself. What if he just threw her out? Now that she'd seen this place, she couldn't just go home. She had to know what this was all about.

Everson drummed his fingers on the table. "There's a substance," he said. "A drug being extracted in Thailand from fossil sites like yours. It's a pheromone that commands submission and obedience. It's incredibly powerful."

"A drug? From sixty-six million year old fossils?"

"Don't ask me how it works. That's not my expertise. But people under its power are effectively enslaved. They will do whatever they're told to do."

"And the United States government wants a supply," Samira said.

"To understand it," Everson said. "To find an antidote. This is some scary stuff, Dr. Shannon. It keeps me up nights, thinking about it in the hands of the Chinese."

"So you don't really want the fossils at all," she said. "You just want the drug. That's why you have guys up there pulverizing priceless fossils."

Everson crossed his arms. "I didn't bring you here for an ethics lecture," he said. "You asked for our reasons; I told you."

"Why does everything have to be about weapons?" Samira asked. "Is it just because men are in charge?"

"Dr. Shannon—"

"No, I don't get it. You find something new and the first thing you think of is, how can I use this to hurt someone else? And the other guys are thinking the exact same thing about you. Instead of trying to understand the people in another country, instead of acknowledging your similarities and trying to see their perspective, all you can think about is killing or controlling them. I've worked with some brilliant and lovely people in China, scientists who care about all the same things I do. They care about truth; they love their children; they want to make things better for humanity. And all you can do is think about how to blow them up."

Gutierrez looked on impassively, but Everson stood, his face red and his jaw clenched.

"I guess this is where you throw me out," Samira said.

Everson met her gaze, but took his time before responding. "No, Dr. Shannon. I'd like to show you something."

She crossed her arms. "Show me what?"

"I'd like to show you what we're up against," he said. "You're so concerned to see what the world looks like from other people's perspectives. I'd like to show you what it looks like from mine."

SAMIRA FOLLOWED him to the sixth floor, with Gutierrez and Everson's assistant, Michelle, following along behind. As they walked down the hallway, Everson said, "Did you know that the Chinese are developing micro-missiles that can fall from space anywhere on Earth?"

"No."

"They're basically tungsten bullets, about the size of a two-liter soda bottle, with a little electronics and fins to steer them as they fall. The Chinese can launch them up there by the bucketload, and then anything they can detect from space, they can guide these little babies into at Mach 10. Boom, no warning, hellfire from the sky. Just one of those things could vaporize a building, sink a carrier, pick an AWACS out of the sky. They've fielded a proof of concept already. We think they're maybe two years from operational, though they've beaten our estimates before. That's classified, by the way—you're cleared for it, but don't go telling CNN."

"Why are you telling me this?"

They reached a serious-looking door, and Everson badged through. He paused before opening it. "Because as much as that keeps me up at night, what I'm about to show you is even scarier."

SAMIRA FOLLOWED him into a large room with a smaller, glass-enclosed space in it. A man and a woman in lab coats sat outside the enclosure at computer terminals, typing. They stopped what they were doing and looked up as Everson came in.

"What is this?" Samira asked.

"A demonstration," Everson said. "Of the most powerful and possibly the most horrifying chemical weapon ever developed. Worse than chlorine gas, worse than phosgene or sarin or other nerve agents. I want you to see what we're trying to combat. Michelle?"

Michelle pressed a button and spoke into a microphone on the wall. "Please continue the experiment."

Inside the glass enclosure were two white men, one in his sixties and one much younger, probably in his twenties. The younger man was well-muscled, had a military haircut, and wore no shirt.

The older man said, "Raise your arms," and the younger man did. The older man lifted a short pole with two metal electrodes at the end and pointed it at the other's bare stomach.

"I'm going to shock you now," the older man said. "You will not move out of the way or stop me."

He moved the prod forward slowly, but the younger man didn't move to avoid it. Besides grimacing and turning his face away, he didn't even flinch. "I'm trying to move," he reported. "Believe me, I'm trying, but I can't. It's not like being paralyzed. It's like I don't even want to move. It's the weirdest feeling. I don't want the pain, but the idea of moving out of the way just seems impossible."

"You should know that Staff Sergeant Bowman volunteered for this duty," Everson said. "He can stop the experiment at any time by saying a safe word."

The prod touched the younger man's stomach with a horrible crackling sound, and he yelled and swore. The older man immediately lifted the prod away, but Samira could see from where she stood that Sergeant Bowman's skin had turned an angry red where it had been touched.

The lab-coated technicians, impassive, typed notes on their computers.

"Okay, raise the voltage," Bowman said. "And keep it there a little longer, will you? I want to see if I can break the hold when I'm actually feeling the pain."

Samira crossed her arms over her chest. "Is this supposed to make me feel *better* about what you're doing here? Some macho display about who can take the most pain? I can watch YouTube if I want to see guys doing stupid things for fun."

"You want to understand other people?" Everson said. "Understand this. The Chinese have this weapon. They've had it for at least a year now. It's my job to make sure they can't use it on us, and I'll tell you, it scares me. We're not beating our chests here and hoping for a fight. We're trying to find an antidote, and so far, we haven't found one."

He ran a hand through his thinning hair. "If I used this and told you to electrocute your sister, you'd do it. If I told you to take your clothes off and dance for us, you might even think it was your idea. And although we haven't tested it, we think you might even kill yourself on command. No amount of sharing kum-ba-ya will stop powerful people from using this now that it exists."

"You said the Chinese have had it for a year. I haven't seen them invading California. Maybe they're like us. Maybe they don't want to use it either."

"We only know they have it because they *are* using it. On their own people, to maintain control, and on others in Southeast Asia, to destabilize governments and raise anti-American sentiment. And no, I'm not naive. I know our government will be likely to use it, too. That's why we need to study it, though. We need an antidote to render it powerless. As far as I'm concerned, that's the first priority of this facility, more than pure science or the development of any other technology."

"Why not go public with it, then?" Samira asked. "Surely the resources of the world's laboratories and scientists will find an antidote faster than you will hidden away here."

Everson looked at her like she was insane. "And in the meantime, every cult leader can have himself a willing harem. Every would-be dictator can gather a loyal army."

"Is it that easy to synthesize?"

"Synthesize? No. If someone ever learns to synthesize this stuff in a lab, the world is in big trouble. But in order to let scientists study it, we'd have to make samples available, and I guarantee, a lot of those samples would get out."

AFTER A FEW MORE ELECTRIC JOLTS, none of which he was able to resist, Staff Sergeant Bowman and the wielder of the cattle prod exited the glass-enclosed area. Bowman walked up to her, still shirtless.

"Hey," he said. "Who's this?"

"I'm Samira Shannon," she said, holding out a hand. She nodded at the red welts on his stomach. "That looks like it hurts."

He shook her hand. "Ah, I can take it. Don't worry about me."

"I'm not worried about you," she said. "I'm worried about this being used by the government on other people."

His grin faltered. "That's above my paygrade, ma'am," he said. "I'm just trying to see what it can do."

Samira turned to Everson, regretting that she had attacked him. He wasn't a bad guy. "You were right," she said. "It is terrifying."

"Give us a chance, Dr. Shannon," he said. "We're trying

to prevent a war, not start one. I wanted you to understand that. We're on the same side."

She met his gaze, evaluating his sincerity. "Okay," she said.

"Okay?"

"Okay. We're on the same side."

Everson held the gaze a little longer and finally nodded. "So, you'll help Captain Gutierrez with his mission?"

"Help him? Are you kidding?" Samira said. "I'm coming along."

Everson laughed. "I'm sorry, that's not on the table."

"It's the only way it can work. I haven't seen the dig since Kit has been working on it. I don't know how far along they are, if they've uncovered another fossil, how it's oriented in the rock, how much of the surrounding layers they've cleared, or anything like that. And there's no way I'm letting some trigger-happy gorillas blow it up with dynamite." She winced at her own choice of words and turned to Gutierrez. "I'm sorry. No offense meant."

"They'll be doing a HALO run," Everson said. "That means jumping out of an airplane at high elevation in complete darkness. There's no way I'm sending a civilian on that kind of mission."

"Actually," Gutierrez said, "I think it's a good idea."

"What?"

"We're all trained for tandem jumping; we'll get her to ground safely. And she's right; none of us will have any idea what we're looking at. I'm not sure I could tell a fossil from ordinary rock. We need an expert."

"She's a civilian, not an agent. I can't send her into the field."

Gutierrez shrugged. "So hire her."

Everson sighed. "I'm going to regret this." He nodded to Samira and shrugged helplessly. "I guess you're hired. Welcome to the team."

CHAPTER EIGHTEEN

Arinya shook Kit awake and shined the light of her phone in his face.

"Wake up," she said. "The king is dead."

He heard the alarm in her voice, but his exhausted brain couldn't process what she was saying. "What king?"

She made a growl of exasperation. "Our king. The king of Thailand. Shot in the night, right there in the palace, and the rest of the royal family with him. They're saying it was American assassins."

Kit shot up out of bed, fully awake now. "The princess?"

There were multiple princesses, but Arinya knew which one he meant. "I don't know. I called the number she gave us, but it went to voicemail."

A wave of dizziness rocked Kit. No one killed the king. The government of Thailand had been overturned countless times, but the royal family had always been there, providing stability as part of a dynasty that had ruled for eight hundred years. Whenever there was a coup, the new leaders would officially inform the king, who would issue a statement recognizing the new leadership. In theory, everything the government did was in the king's name. Most new governments gave themselves credibility by claiming they had taken control in order to uphold the monarchy. The king himself didn't actually run the government, though. Why would the Americans assassinate him?

Unless...

The more likely truth crashed into his brain. What if the king had refused to give his blessing to General Wattana's new government? The king was one of the three pillars of Thai civilization; if he opposed the new regime, Wattana's power, even over the military, would be in serious jeopardy. It would be in even more jeopardy if people knew he had assassinated the king, but the American assassin story fed into people's fears enough that most would probably accept it. And those who didn't would stay quiet.

Kit had been a boy the last time a Thai king had died. All businesses in Thailand had been closed for a week, and great mountains of white flowers had filled all the public buildings in Bangkok. Every billboard advertisement in the city had been replaced with memorial statements and pictures, and every newspaper and TV channel carried no other news.

If Wattana really had killed the king, it was the worst sort of heresy and treason. If the royal family was gone...it was like there was no more Thailand.

Kit felt a growing sense of panic. "What can we do?"

Of course, they could do nothing. They were a pair of paleontologists, far from the halls of power, who had been fortunate enough to meet the princess once. He desperately hoped she was safe, but he couldn't protect her. She would be heading for Bangkok now, he had no doubt, with far larger concerns than a green chemical from the Cretaceous.

A sharp report echoed through the room, rattling the glassware. Kit ducked.

Arinya's eyes grew wide. "Was that a gunshot?"

They heard shouting in the hallway. "Should we hide?" Kit asked.

"Where? Under the tables?" The tables were tall and offered no concealment.

The door banged open and Lieutenant Somjai rushed in. He looked terrified. "Is there another way out of here?"

Arinya shook her head. "What's happening?"

"It's the Red Wa," he said. "Run if you can."

He turned and rushed out, but almost immediately backed into the room again, a gun pointed in his face. Holding the gun and following him into the room was a muscular Thai kid, maybe eighteen or nineteen years old, with tattooed arms and a nose ring. "Where you going, grandfather?" the kid said.

Somjai backed up, crying out in fear. Kit was surprised at the lieutenant's abject terror until a familiar scent reached him and he started to tremble as well. It was a core, animal sensation, based not on the kid's gun or sadistic smile but on a deep certainty that he could not be resisted.

Three more young men ran into the room, lean and hard, wearing T-shirts with the sleeves torn off to display their muscular arms. All of them held handguns. "The soldiers are *gone*," said one, leaving no doubt as to what he meant by the phrase. "These here are all that's left."

The kid with the nose ring spread his arms wide. "So this must be the lab."

"Please," Somjai said, dropping to his knees. "Take whatever you want."

The kid sneered down at him. "Disgusting," he said. With exaggerated casualness, he turned his gun sideways and shot Somjai in the head. The noise boomed through the cinderblock room, battering Kit's ears. The lieutenant collapsed to the ground.

Kit couldn't believe it. They'd just *shot* the man, for no reason, right there on the floor. His brain wanted to shut down and make this go away. He started hyperventilating and couldn't stop.

The leader paced, waving his gun around. "We hear

you've been digging up things that belong to us," he said. "We're going to take everything you have here. You won't go back to that spot you've been digging, either; that's ours now."

Kit didn't want to call attention to himself, but the fear was in his nostrils, and defensive words just spilled out. "We're no threat. We can help you."

"Shut up," the kid said. Kit's throat tightened, and he found that he couldn't make a sound. He couldn't even grunt.

"You can't help me, but I bet she can." The kid turned his attention to Arinya and whistled softly. "Ain't she a nice one. You'll help me out, won't you?"

Arinya, her face strained in fear, nodded.

"Come on over here."

She made her way around the table and stood in front of him. The kid's cronies circled her, leering.

"You're going to help me out, and then you're going to help each of my boys out, aren't you?"

She nodded again, her eyes locked with his.

"Good girl. Start by taking that shirt off, so we can get a proper look at you."

To Kit's horror, Arinya complied, starting to unbutton her blouse. He couldn't let this happen. He had to do something. One of the kids had his back to Kit now. They seemed to have forgotten about him. If he could grab the kid's gun quickly enough, then maybe...

"Whoa, hey now," the leader said. He had seen Kit step forward. "Don't you move. It's your lucky day. You get to watch."

Kit tried to dart forward and go for the gun anyway, but his body wouldn't respond. Instead of moving forward, he just shook, overcome by a paralyzing fear. Arinya had her blouse open now, exposing pale skin and a simple white bra. *No*, Kit thought. He tried to master his will. It was just a smell. Just chemicals. He was no prey animal to be so easily cowed. He could overcome this. But try as he might, he couldn't move.

Arinya pulled her arms out of her blouse. She'd never looked so vulnerable and small. The kid with the nose ring took a step closer, eyeing her appreciatively. He dipped a finger into the spreading pool of blood by Lieutenant Somjai's body and then smeared it idly along the line of her jaw, over her chin, and down her neck to her chest, leaving a trail of red. He licked his lips. "That's a good girl," he said. "Now take off the rest and we'll have some fun."

A new scent reached Kit's nostrils, stronger than the other, but before he could think about it, Arinya lunged forward. She grabbed the leader's nose ring and yanked hard. It came out easily and fell to the ground, not a ring at all, but a half-circle of plastic connecting two long cylinders. Nose plugs. In the same motion, she stuffed her blouse into his face and shouted, "On your knees! Drop the gun!"

To Kit's astonishment, the kid fell to his knees. The gun clattered to the floor.

"The rest of you!" Arinya shouted. "On your knees and drop your weapons!" Kit found himself falling to his knees with the others, and only then did he understand what had happened. Arinya had applied the high-ranking dominance chemical to her blouse. The leader had worn a pair of nose plugs to protect himself from anyone employing the same trick. His cronies hadn't, possibly because he was dominating them as well. Arinya's scent, however, had been stronger, or at least communicated a higher rank, and once it had spread through the room, they had obeyed her instead.

Arinya put her blouse back on, her face contorted in rage. She faced down the leader, who remained meekly on his knees. "Hands on your head," she commanded.

He complied.

"Spread your legs."

He shifted his knees apart.

"Don't move," she said, and kicked him between the legs. He bellowed in pain, but didn't move or try to protect himself.

"You wanted to have some fun," she said, her eyes flashing. "I thought that was fun. But I think you wanted your friends to have some fun, too, didn't you?" She pointed at one of the other thugs. "Your turn," she said. "Kick him hard as you can."

The kid stood and did as she asked. He wore army boots and was stronger than Arinya. His kick lifted the leader into the air and sent him sprawling on the floor, whimpering. "Don't go anywhere," she told him. "Everybody wants a turn."

She scooped up a gun from the floor and shoved the barrel into the leader's crotch. "Feels different on this side, doesn't it? Not so much fun now. Well, I'm going to make sure you never do this to anyone ever again."

"Arinya!" Kit said. "Don't!"

She whirled on him, eyes like daggers. "Don't you dare tell me what I can't do."

"These are violent men. You've already won. You don't have to stoop to their level."

"You think I'm the first woman he's done this to? You think if I let him go, I'll be the last? No, this kind of man doesn't learn from his mistakes. He'll go right out and hurt women all the more just to get his pride back. I won't let that happen."

She fired. The kid on the ground screamed and writhed. She put a second bullet in his head, silencing him. Then she systematically shot each of the other men. They dropped to the floor one by one, offering no resistance.

Kit gaped. "Arinya! You—"

The gun swung again and pointed at him. Arinya's face was flushed, her eyes wide, her face and neck still smeared with blood. More blood spattered her blouse from the men she had shot.

"I wanted to protect you," he said. Tears streamed down his face. "I couldn't move."

She lowered the gun. "You couldn't help it," she said. "You would have done anything they told you to do."

"How did you resist?"

She pulled a glistening wad of cotton out of one nostril and then the other, tossing them to the floor.

"You were in control the whole time," he said. "You just pretended to obey to get close enough."

The door opened. Kit cringed, thinking it would be more of the Red Wa, but a big man in a black suit entered instead —Mongkut, the princess's bodyguard, followed by the princess herself. Mai took in the scene and seemed to understand it completely.

"So it begins," she said. To Arinya: "You have what we need?"

"I've got it," she said.

They seemed to be expecting each other. Kit was left gaping, still trying to catch up. "What are you doing here?"

It occurred to Kit that since their visit, Arinya must have spoken further to Mai without telling him. They certainly seemed to be understanding one another now.

Arinya looked at him. "You can come with us if you want," she said. "Just don't try to stop us."

"What are you going to do?"

"This chemical you've found, it's a miracle," Mai said. "In the right hands, it could save the world."

"That's what you're going to do? Save the world?"

Mai glanced with disdain at the bodies surrounding her on the floor. "I don't know about the whole world. But we'll start by making Thailand a little bit better."

She nodded to Arinya, who tucked the handgun into her pants and then collected all of the spray bottles from the table into a bag. Mai walked out with Mongkut right behind her. Arinya followed wIthout a backward glance at Kit or the men she had killed.

Kit stared after them for a moment. He heard a siren in

the distance. There was nothing left for him here, and the police were no sanctuary. Even if they believed him, they were probably already bought by the Red Wa. If they detained him, he wouldn't last the night. Kit jumped to his feet and ran after Arinya and Mai.

CHAPTER NINETEEN

P ak started to think he might get away with it.

After freeing the girl, he'd driven back to Tachileik, expecting to be killed. The Red Wa had accountants and computer records like any other business, keeping careful stock of every ounce of illegal drugs that passed through their hands. He assumed they did the same with the girls they trafficked, but perhaps they didn't keep records of people the same way. Or perhaps the girl's ancestors were watching out for him now. Whatever the reason, no one in Tachileik ever asked him about the girl. They didn't seem to realize she was missing.

Until today. He was in the mess hall eating a bowl of gai yang when Decha, one of Ukrit's enforcers, sat down across from him. That could have been coincidence, until another enforcer sat down on the bench right next to Pak, blocking his escape. He swallowed painfully. They had finally caught up with him.

"Had a chat with Kulap from Chiang Mai," Decha said. He was impressively muscled, with elaborate tattoos covering his face. "Says he sent a girl with his last shipment to pay off his debt."

"That so?" Pak said. He put another piece of chicken in his mouth, trying not to show his fear. It was a mistake. His throat had closed up too tightly for him to swallow.

"Girl never arrived," Decha said.

Pak didn't reply. He was trying to decide if he should spit the chicken back into his bowl.

Decha slammed a hand down on the table, making Pak jump. "Kulap swears he put her in the truck and watched the driver leave. Turns out that driver was you."

Pak's mind raced through all the lies he could tell, but nothing seemed remotely believable. He just sat there, the chicken sitting like a lead weight on his tongue. He thought he'd gotten used to the idea of dying, but now that the moment was actually here, he was terrified. Tomorrow would come, and he wouldn't be here to see it. He might not even make it off of this bench.

Decha pulled a knife from his belt and pointed it at Pak's face. "When I speak, you better answer," he said. "You want to tell me what happened to that girl?"

Pak spat the chicken back into his bowl. Decha made a disgusted noise. "I'm going to cut you until there's nothing left to cut," he said. He pulled back the knife to slash at Pak's face, then stopped, looking over Pak's shoulder. The mess hall went quiet. Hesitantly, Pak turned away from Decha to see what was going on.

A woman walked down the aisle between the rows of benches. That was odd. Women weren't allowed here during the day. Was she one of Ukrit's mistresses? She was young and pretty, but she didn't dress like they did. If she wasn't Ukrit's, she was taking her life in her hands walking through the camp like this. Where had she come from? As she passed, he caught a scent that reminded him of Ukrit, a scent that filled him with fear. Maybe she was his, then.

But wait, he recognized her from the television! It was the

Princess Sirindhorn. What did she think she was doing, coming here like this? These men would tear her apart.

Pak's sense of fear grew. When the princess reached the front, she turned and faced them all, her bearing proud, nothing like the cowed and beaten women that Ukrit and his men used until they tired of them.

"*Sawatdi kha,*" the princess said politely. "Who is the man in charge here?"

"I am!" someone said to nervous laughter, but others called out Ukrit's name. The voices that spoke sounded anxious, afraid.

"Where can I find him?"

Someone pointed her the way to Ukrit's house.

"Thank you," she said with a *wai*. "You should know that Ukrit is no longer in charge of this camp. I am. If any of you have ever killed a woman or used a woman for sex against her will, you will kill yourself right now. The rest of you will come with me."

To Pak's astonishment, weapons pulled free of their holsters all around the room. Any thought that they might have been meant to challenge the princess's claims vanished as dozens of deafening shots fired and body after body slumped to the floor. Decha turned his knife around and slit his own throat.

Pak wanted to run in terror, but he found that he couldn't. The princess had said to follow her. He rose to his feet and, with the rest of the survivors, followed her out into the bright sun.

KIT STARED about the mess hall in satisfaction. A small piece of him recognized that yesterday he would have been horrified, and that this new feeling was driven by the fact that he, too, was inhaling Mai's scent. But he didn't care. These were violent men who had probably committed horrible atrocities. Mai had just single-handedly done more to combat the Red Wa than either the Thai or Burmese governments had in years. She was an avenging angel, and he adored her for it.

"Why didn't you kill them all?" Arinya asked.

"I didn't kill any of them," Mai said. "They judged themselves for their crimes. I just told them what the penalty should be."

The surviving men gathered around. "This is dangerous," Kit said. "You can't keep them all in range of your scent forever. All it takes is someone with a long-range rifle—or a nose plug, for that matter—and that's the end. Not to mention that you're going to run out of spray."

A thought struck him: what if Mai had no intention of making it last? If this was a suicide mission, then what would happen to him? Nothing good, that was for sure.

"You, you, and you," Mai said, pointing to three of the toughest-looking soldiers. "You're my bodyguards. Don't let anyone hurt me or my friends Arinya and Kit here. Now where are the weapons kept?"

Twenty minutes later, their adhoc army outfitted with AK-47s and body armor, Mai advanced on Ukrit's house. They took out the two guards in a burst of gunfire and Mai and her bodyguards went inside with Kit trailing nervously behind. Ukrit came running down the stairs in a pair of boxer shorts, a pistol in his hand. He was middle-aged, with a muscular build, bald head, and cheeks that drooped in pronounced jowls.

"Drop it," Mai said.

Protected with a nose plug, Ukrit raised the pistol instead. Misinterpreting who was in charge, he fired on one of Mai's bodyguards, taking him down. The others lit up the room with their automatic rifles, sending splinters flying and riddling Ukrit's body with bullets.

"Check upstairs," Arinya told Kit. "He was probably with

a girl."

Kit did as he was told, and found that Arinya was right. A young girl screamed and covered herself when she saw him. Kit spoke softly, wrapped her in a blanket, and led her downstairs.

"We'll find a lot more girls before this is done," Mai said. "We'll need counselors and investigators to find out where they came from."

Kit's mind reeled. "How?" he said. "Where will we get counselors and investigators? We can't take on all of organized crime singlehanded."

"That's why no one ever tries," Mai said. "Everyone thinks, 'I can't fight it, so I might as well just take this bribe, because the alternative is just getting myself killed.' Well, this is our chance. We're going to turn it all around. Now"—she turned to her bodyguards—"show me where the drug labs are."

THAT NIGHT WAS the scariest night of Kit's life. Mai and Arinya both somehow managed to sleep soundly, but Kit kept expecting armed criminals to burst into the house at any moment and gun them down. Mai had taken control of the drug labs with ease, uncovering large quantities of the domination spray. Where had they gotten so much? They must have found dozens of maniraptor fossil caches and pulverized the bones to extract the liquid. Kit mourned for the lost research data. Arinya, however, showed the workers her method for refining the drug from the fossil liquid, which was apparently superior to the method they had been using.

It was amazing how easily Mai had taken over the town. She seemed confident, but Kit worried. Taking over was the easy part. As long as she remained close enough to smell, they would obey her. But what happened when they moved out of range? What would happen now that she was asleep? Keeping control over everyone across time and distance seemed impossible. She told him not to worry, that they had all seen her power in the mess hall, and fear would keep them in line at least for the night. He wasn't so sure.

He must have slept eventually, because when he opened his eyes, light streamed through the windows and Mai stood there, unharmed. She had donned the dark green uniform of the United Wa State Army and tied a red cloth around her neck. She opened the door, and her bodyguards—new ones now, she must have sent the others to sleep—lifted their rifles and stood at attention.

"Let's go," she said. "It's going to be a busy day."

CHAPTER TWENTY

"Where on Earth have you been?" Beth stood at the stove, pushing vegetables around in a wok. The smell of stir fry filled the apartment.

"Doing some research," Samira said. "At the university."

"You're a terrible liar," Beth said without turning around.

A knot tightened in Samira's gut. This was impossible. How was she supposed to keep all this a secret from Beth? "I've been looking at our photos," she said. "We still might be able to get some data we could work with. Enough to write a paper, probably."

Beth glanced at her, then back down at the sizzling wok. "I'm not going to let this go. You might as well tell me now and get it over with."

Samira peered over her shoulder at the stir fry. "Wow, where'd you get Isan sausage?"

"Asian market over in Thornton," Beth said, dropping the spoon and crossing her arms. "Fine. If you won't tell me, I'll guess. Let me know how close I get. You were all fired up about the CIA maybe getting our fossils stolen. So you found the guy who invested in our project, camped out in his office, and threatened to tell the press unless he told you all his secrets. How am I doing?"

Samira deflated. "I *told* him I wouldn't be able to keep it from you."

Beth faced her. "I was right?"

"Close enough. I didn't have to threaten him. He wanted to tell me, or someone wanted him to. But they said I couldn't tell you. They made me sign all kinds of papers saying they'd put me in jail if I did."

"I don't get it," Beth said. "What could possibly be so secret?"

"I don't know, not really. They seem to think there's some kind of chemical trapped with our fossils that they can use. But it doesn't make any sense. Organic chemicals break down after that much time."

"What do they want from you?"

Samira didn't answer.

"Come on, Sami. You know I'll get it out of you."

She sighed. "They want to go to Thailand and take the fossils."

"But they were destroyed. That Thai colonel took a sledgehammer to them."

"He's Chinese, apparently. But no, not those. Kit's been working the site since we left. They said he dug down to the next maniraptor already. They want to go and steal that one."

"From Kit?"

"From the Chinese. If it's that valuable, they aren't going to let Kit keep it. They think Kit might be working under duress."

"And they want you to go along?"

Samira laughed. "Not exactly. They just wanted me to tell them how to get it out safely. I had to bully them into letting me go."

Beth took her by the shoulders, her face incredulous.

"You're going back to Thailand with some CIA secret agents to steal back our fossils?"

"Special ops team. But yeah."

"Okay," Beth said. "When do we leave?"

Samira looked up, horrified. "Beth, you can't come. You can't even tell them I told you. They'll bury me in a dungeon somewhere and throw away the key. Besides, it's dangerous."

Beth dropped her hands and stepped back. "And what, I don't care about those fossils as much as you do? You're allowed to risk your life, but I'm not? That's my research, too. I got thrown out of the country, just like you did. I might not show it as much, but I'm just as pissed about what happened as you are."

"They won't let you come."

Beth gave her a winning smile. "I'm sure you can convince them."

SAMIRA DROVE up the gravel road, dust billowing around the car. Everson and Gutierrez were waiting with a group of soldiers in fatigues, all of them young and physically fit, with military haircuts and chiseled features. Samira stopped the car, pulled the parking brake, and then stepped out of the car. From the passenger side, Beth stepped out as well.

Everson pulled off his sunglasses. He stepped forward, waving them at Beth but looking at Samira. "What the hell is this?"

"I'm sorry," Samira said, "There was no keeping it from her."

"Miss Shannon!"

"Doctor."

Everson looked like he was about to explode. "*Doctor* Shannon, you signed papers. You promised not to tell anyone what you knew on pain of imprisonment or even death. I was quite explicit that this restriction included your sister."

"She knew! I couldn't help it. The minute I got home she knew something was up. How could I possibly disappear and not tell her what was going on?"

"This is what we *do*," Gutierrez snarled. "That's what a secret mission *is*. We don't tell our families, and if things go south and we die, they never get to know why."

"If you can trust me, you can trust her," Samira said. "We're practically twins."

Everson looked back and forth between Samira, dark-skinned and six feet tall, and Beth, pale, blonde, and barely five-foot-two. "Twins," he said.

"I want to come," Beth said. "It can only help you to have a second expert on hand."

"A second untrained child to keep from getting killed," Gutierrez said.

Everson held up a hand, considering. "She goes," he finally said. Gutierrez started to object, but Everson cut him off. "If one of them gets shot, you'll have a backup. She goes."

"Thank you," Samira said.

Everson rounded on her. "Don't think this is over. Operational security is something we take seriously around here. You were extended the trust of the United States government, and you violated that trust. There will be consequences."

"Provided I don't get shot," Samira said.

"Oh, I hope you don't," Everson retorted. "I want to shoot you myself when you get back."

CHAPTER TWENTY-ONE

To Kit's surprise, the soldiers' loyalty to Mai lasted long beyond the time when they actually breathed her scent. Far from feeling like they were controlled against their will, they seemed to retell the story of their lives so that following the princess was what they had always wanted. He overheard soldiers saying they had dreamed that she would come, or expressing long-held hatred for the sex trafficking they were all involved in. She was their savior.

And why not? Kit thought of her the same way. He had always loved his country, but hated the organized crime that operated unchecked. On his own, though, he would never have done anything about it. She was saving not only him, but their whole country.

At Arinya's instructions, they moved the women and girls they found into Ukrit's house to be protected from harm until she could get them better care. They burned the heroin and methamphetamines far from the town.

Despite the newfound loyalty of their drug runner army, they would need more of the domination chemical if they were going to make it very far. The rest of the Red Wa in Pangkham would hear about this coup, and they wouldn't be happy about losing a major center for their operations. If the Chinese Ministry of State Security had been funding Ukrit to get their hands on the domination chemical, they might come calling as well.

They'd found Ukrit's stash, a dozen vials of refined liquid, as well as some fossils in various stages of processing. It wouldn't be enough. They were already burning through it at a rapid pace. They couldn't afford to run out.

"We need to get back to Kalasin," Kit told Arinya. "There's a lot more chemical at the dig site. How long do you think it will take the colonel to conscript another team to extract it?"

"I've told her the same thing," Arinya said. "She's trying to consolidate her power here, to make sure things don't go right back to the way they were when she leaves."

"Then send us. Give us a little chemical and a dozen soldiers; we'll come back with ten times as much. A hundred times."

"I'll talk to her."

"I'll come with you."

They found Princess Sirindhorn sitting on the floor in Ukrit's living room. The room was packed with women sharing a meal of *app mu* and sticky rice. "This town belongs to you now," Mai was telling them. "No man can tell you what to do, not anymore."

"I want to go home," one girl said. She looked no older than fifteen.

"We will help you do that," Mai said. "I've contacted some doctors, female doctors I know who care about our cause, and therapists as well. They are on their way here to help. For those of you who want to go back to your home towns, we'll help you do that as soon as possible. For those of you who don't want to, or have nothing to go back to, you are welcome to work for me here."

"How?" one woman asked. "I don't know anything about drugs."

"The drug trade is over," Mai said. "We're going to rebuild this town and many more. All of these men who have spent their lives exploiting others are now going to work to make that happen. They're going to work for you."

One of the younger girls started to cry. Mai touched her cheek. "Slowly, slowly," she told the girl. "Healing first. Rest. You don't need to do anything until you truly believe you are safe." She addressed all of them. "Your lives are different now. Believe it. In time it will be true."

"Princess," Arinya said. "A word."

Mai nodded. "Eat," she told the women. "Talk with each other and rest."

She joined Arinya and Kit at the side of the room. Arinya told her what they wanted to do.

"Go," Mai said. "Take the men you need and do what you can. I can't leave yet. There's word of a Red Wa force heading our way from Mong Lin, ten times as strong as what we have here."

Kit gasped. "What are you going to do? You can't fight so many."

"Of course not," Mai said. "We will surrender."

Kit couldn't believe it. "After all this? You're just giving up?"

Her smile left him half in love with her. "Not even close."

SAMIRA AND BETH traveled with the special ops team in a military truck that allowed no view of the outside. On the way, a Master Sergeant drilled them on every moment of the planned operation. The only way in and out was by air. The dig site was two hundred miles from the ocean across inhospitable, mountainous terrain. They would parachute in, and once they had the fossil, they would be extracted by helicopter to a cruiser waiting off the coast of Vietnam.

"I won't lie to you," the sergeant said. "This is a complicated op. We will be dropping at night over enemy territory. The target site may be guarded. We'll land a few miles away and approach silently, leaving you behind with our equipment until we've cleared the site."

"I've never jumped out of an airplane before," Beth said. "Pretty sure Samira hasn't either."

"You'll be tandem jumping with two of us," the sergeant said. "Each man is assigned a load of equipment to carry, and the two of you are just part of that. Don't worry, we'll keep you safe."

Despite assuring them that they wouldn't need to do anything on the jump, the sergeant spent the next half hour going over the equipment in great detail and teaching them how to jump safely.

Eventually, they reached a military base—Samira had no idea which one—and boarded a plane for the flight across the Pacific. The crossing was even worse than the passenger flight they'd taken home, with less accommodations and no in-flight movie to distract her. It started to occur to her that this was real. She was about to invade another country with a team of special forces to steal something that might be guarded by real soldiers firing real bullets. The fact that she didn't consider it theft—she had a contract from the Thai government for those fossils, after all—didn't change the risk. She started to wonder if this had been a really bad idea.

The plane landed on an island somewhere. Oahu? Guam? She had no clue. They were shuffled onto another plane and took off again. She started to lose track of what day it was. When they landed again and boarded yet another plane, Samira wanted to scream from the sleep deprivation and tension. The stress was going to kill her before the bullets ever did.

"This is unbearable," Beth said. "Just throw me out of the plane already."

When the moment actually came, it happened fast. Before she knew it, Samira was standing in front of an open door, buffeted by frigid air, swathed in black and strapped to the front of a staff sergeant with massive biceps and thighs as big as her waist. Beth was similarly strapped to another soldier. One moment they were standing in front of Samira, and the next, with a tiny shriek from Beth, they were gone.

No, Samira thought. *This is insane. I'm not doing this.*

They jumped. Samira gasped as they fell free of the plane. Wind tore past her face. She fought to breathe. The air was cold and thin, and it seemed to be snatched out of her lungs the moment she tried to pull it in. Tears streamed from her eyes.

The ground below was almost entirely black, the darkness broken only by a few tiny lights and the faint glow of distant towns. They hurtled toward it. Somehow she had imagined it would feel like flying. It just felt like falling to her death.

They fell and fell, streaking towards the ground, until Samira was certain something had gone wrong with the chute. She could barely see anything, but surely the ground couldn't be that far away. She knew the plan was to jump high to avoid detection and then not open the chutes until the last moment. Still, she tensed, expecting at any moment to break every bone in her body colliding into the Khorat plateau.

Instead, a sudden jerk seemed to yank her up in the air by the straps. She barely managed not to scream. She could just make out the black edges of the parachute above them. Then, finally, she saw the arid ground of the plateau, rushing toward them much too fast. She immediately forgot everything she'd been told about proper landing technique and pulled her body into a fetal position. Fortunately, the soldier she was strapped to executed a flawless landing fall, collapsing to the ground and rolling with his arms wrapped around her.

The soldier unstrapped her, and she stood, wobbling a bit. Beth stood not far away, her eyes wide. Samira counted heads. The entire team had landed safely within the drop zone.

One by one, the soldiers ghosted into the night, leaving Samira and Beth behind with two of the soldiers and all of their equipment. Nothing to do now but catch her breath and wait.

CHAPTER TWENTY-TWO

Samira waited in the dark, terrified, until the soldiers returned to tell them the site was clear.

"The place is empty," Gutierrez said. "Not a single guard. Given the value of this site, that's a bit creepy. I'm going to send out some scouts to give us warning in case this is an ambush."

He held out two gas masks for Samira and Beth.

"What are we supposed to do with those?" Samira asked.

The full force of Gutierrez's expression was lost behind his own mask, but she picked up on the disdain anyway. "You wear them."

"We've been working this site for months, and we never wore masks before."

"And tonight you will wear them," Gutierrez said. "Non-negotiable."

Samira sighed and took the mask. Beth did as well, and the two of them followed Gutierrez into the night.

As they approached the site, despite the darkness, Samira began to make out familiar landmarks. A thrill of adrenaline rushed through her. She'd been afraid they would never see this place again, and now they were back. She felt like a tomb robber, creeping in under cover of darkness to steal valuable artifacts, but she'd done the honest work in the daylight. It was Colonel Zhanwei who had stolen from her.

The special ops team had carried an incredible amount of equipment down with them. They pulled out black pouches that expanded into cloth shades taller than Samira, arranged around the site to block the light. Samira and Beth pulled on gas masks and head-mounted flashlights with red filters. An eerie crimson light illuminated the stone.

"Wow," Beth said. "Kit's been busy."

She was right. The site was substantially more developed than when they'd left it. A layer of hillside had been removed, including the first row of maniraptor skeletons she'd seen in the GPR scan. She estimated eight of the twenty-seven she'd originally seen had been removed with incredible haste. Each of those skeletons should have been the work of a full season. Of course, she couldn't really fault him. She was about to yank out as much as she could in a single night.

"They say he was probably coerced," Samira said. "I think we've moved beyond what's best for science."

Gutierrez appeared at her side. "Tell my men what to do," he said. "Our helo evac will be here in three hours. It's a long flight, so they won't have the fuel to hang around waiting. When they arrive, we go, with the prize or without it."

"I understand," Samira said. "Give us ten minutes to understand what we're looking at, and we'll give you our best shot."

Gutierrez gave her a rock hard stare. "Ten minutes," he said. "Not a second more."

He disappeared on the other side of the cloth shield where the soldiers who weren't scouting surrounded them for protection. Samira and Beth were left alone at the site.

"We need to find where the next row starts," Samira said. "Ideally, we take out one skeleton whole, with all of the surrounding rock."

"Even if that means potentially damaging the skeletons to either side?" Beth asked.

Samira shrugged, wincing. "We'll do the best we can. But yeah, that's probably what it will take."

They set to work with chisels and hammers, pounding away at a reckless speed to find the edges of the next row of skeletons. Rock debris crumbled away and collected at their feet. In a few minutes, they had uncovered enough chocolate brown fossil ridges to confirm their memories of the location and orientation of the bones.

Samira was just about to call Gutierrez back when a chisel tap by Beth sent a thin sheet of rock sliding away to shatter into pieces. Samira froze, staring at what lay underneath. She heard Beth's chisel clatter to the ground. A vein of rich green marked the rock, a translucent river like a chunk of amber the color of emerald. Visible inside the thick green crystal was a maniraptor head. Not a skull. A head, with dark brown skin, a gaping jaw filled with teeth, and *feathers*, beautifully preserved protofeathers like a fan of hollow filaments, not yet evolved into the branching barbules of modern birds.

Samira and Beth stared at it, frozen with astonishment. Nothing like this had ever been found before. Tail feathers of small dinosaurs had been found preserved in amber. Woolly rhinos and mammoths had been found preserved in ice, but those were tens of thousands of years old, not tens of millions. Samira nearly cried at the beauty of it. What they were looking at was impossible.

"This is what we're taking with us," Samira said. "This right here."

"How far back does it go?" Beth asked.

They peered into the green substance, but at more than half a meter deep, it became too cloudy to make out any details.

"GPR showed complete skeletons," Samira said. "Let's assume it's all there and blow it out accordingly."

The surface of the green had smeared, making it harder to see the dinosaur preserved inside. Beth touched it with a tentative finger. "We're losing it," she said. "Whatever this stuff is, it doesn't stay crystalized in contact with the air."

"We'll have to do this quickly."

With the help of Gutierrez and two explosives specialists from the drop team, they drilled holes in the surrounding rock and planted them with tiny, shaped charges. "I hate this," Beth said. "Any kind of vibration risks damaging the surrounding fossils."

"You won't ever get your hands on the other fossils anyway," Gutierrez said.

"I still don't want to see them damaged. These are valuable to science for all of humanity, not just to any one person or country."

"Take what you can get," Gutierrez said. "It's this way or nothing."

"I get it," Beth said. "But I don't have to like it."

They retreated behind the black shades and took shelter behind an outcropping. The red lights strapped to their foreheads didn't ruin their night vision like white light would have, but the Kalasin night was still deep black, with only the glorious vista of the stars above to illuminate anything. One of the explosive specialists pressed a button, and the charges blew with a muted *whump*, followed by the patter of rock chips raining down on the hillside.

They rushed back to find that the explosives had done their work: a section the size of a small car had detached from the surrounding rock. Soldiers scrambled behind it and tried, unsuccessfully, to shift it.

"It's too big," Gutierrez said. "That thing must weigh thirty tons. No way we're lifting that out of here."

Samira climbed over the rock and checked the newly-exposed back side. More green crystal, this time revealing the slope of a protofeather-covered tail. Her heart pounded in her chest. There was an *entire preserved maniraptor* in there, muscles and skin and feathers included. This find blew away what they'd uncovered before. It blew away what any paleontologist had ever uncovered before.

"It's the green crystal we need," she told Gutierrez. "It's probably lighter than the sandstone. Blow away the rock on either side, and we might get it small enough."

"We don't have much time," Gutierrez told his explosive specialists. "Get it done."

They drilled the holes and sheltered again while the explosives detonated. Samira barely waited for the shards to stop falling. She pushed past the shades with rock dust still raining down into her hair. Her headlamp revealed a block almost entirely composed of translucent green material, now toppled onto its side. Embedded in the green was a thing not seen for sixty-six million years: a fully-formed theropod dinosaur, as perfectly preserved as the day it had died.

The green material, however, was deteriorating fast. The surface was slick and vapor poured off the edges. In one place, green liquid was actually dripping onto the ground.

"Get it covered in plastic!" Samira shouted to the first soldier to come through. "As airtight as possible."

The team pulled out a roll of plastic they'd brought for the purpose—not as good as the plaster casts they usually packed fossils in, but a good deal faster and lighter—and began rolling it around the green block as if wrapping up food for the refrigerator.

Gutierrez's two-way radio crackled. "Sir, we've got multiple vehicles incoming, two minutes to your south."

He lifted the radio to his mouth and pressed a button. "Copy that. The welcome party is ready. Get yourself back here, over." He lowered the radio. "Time's up, people. We've got company."

CHAPTER TWENTY-THREE

K it and Arinya rode at the head of a line of Isuzu pickup trucks, following country roads back toward Khai Nun. The men following them, soldiers in the Red Wa army, came from all over South East Asia. They were soldiers in the sense that they carried automatic rifles and weren't afraid to use them, though most of their experience was in threatening unarmed people rather than disciplined fighting techniques. Given the number of rivals and factions within the Red Wa, they had probably seen combat at some point, but if they had to go up against the Chinese military, it wouldn't be an even fight.

Kit's main worry wasn't the Chinese, though. He worried that the men following him would decide it was easier to shoot him and Arinya in the back than to obey their orders. They had a tiny amount of the domination chemical with them, but not enough to control all of these men for days. He would have to rely on their continued loyalty to Mai, and the ingrained belief that in the Red Wa, to disobey orders meant violent death.

The drive to Khai Nun took fourteen hours. Arinya drove their vehicle most of the time, though Kit took some turns along the way. They could have told one of the men to drive, of course, but Kit preferred the freedom to speak frankly with Arinya without an armed drug runner listening in. He also preferred that if the men decided to go rogue along the way, they could do it without bringing Kit and Arinya along.

When they stopped for gas or food, the men just took what they liked from stores, confident in their guns and reputation to cow any resistance. The locals knew better than to call the cops. Kit cringed to be causing such fear and hardship, but he reminded himself that these things had gone on long before his involvement, and the whole reason he was here was to stop it from happening in the future.

By the time they reached Kalasin province, Kit was exhausted from the endless ride and constant tension. The plan was to set up tents on the plateau and start work in the morning. He had contacted his students at Nakhon Ratchasima to come and help. The thugs with guns were there to defend them against the colonel and his forces, not to assist with the work.

The plan changed when they stopped the vehicles and heard the clear sound of explosives from the direction of the hills.

"The Chinese," Kit said. "They're already at the site." He shouted instructions to the men and the vehicles roared to life again. Arinya restarted the truck, and they took off toward the site. As they jounced along the rough road, Kit felt every muscle in his body tightening in fear. Shouldn't the men with guns be leading the charge? But of course, only he and Arinya knew where they were going. He concentrated on the idea of Chinese soldiers tearing up his dig site with explosives, trying to turn his fear into anger. It didn't work.

Automatic fire tore through the night behind them. Behind them? Kit twisted in his seat, but he couldn't see what was happening. He leaned out of the open window instead and looked back. Several vehicles in their caravan had fallen behind. The darkness lit up with muzzle flashes and another one veered sharply and skidded to a halt, its tires blown out. They'd driven straight into an ambush.

The men opened fire, painting the darkness in hopes of hitting their invisible enemy. There were shouts as bullets pinged off the trucks and two men fell. Kit realized that he was presenting himself as an easy target and ducked back inside.

"Keep driving!" he shouted. "Away from the site. Get us out of here."

The sounds of weapons fire and shouting increased. Arinya punched the accelerator, veering off-road and away from the battle. Before they'd made it a hundred meters, a shadow in black rose up from the brush and fired a rifle at them. Kit heard a pop as their right front tire ruptured, sending the vehicle swerving to the right. Arinya tried to power through it despite the rough terrain, but the next shot shattered their windshield. She screamed and slammed on the brakes.

"Get out and put your hands up," she told him. "I've got this."

Kit did as she said, shouting in both Mandarin and Thai that they were unarmed. He could smell the sweet petroleum scent that meant Arinya had used some of the domination liquid, but it wasn't going to help. The two men that approached them from either side wore gas masks along with night vision goggles and dark green fatigues. Despite not being able to see their faces, it was immediately apparent to Kit that these soldiers were too tall to be Thai or Chinese. When they shouted at them in English to get down on the ground, his suspicion was confirmed. Americans.

How had the Americans gotten here? How did they even know there was something of value here to be taken?

The soldiers roughly checked them for weapons and zip tied their hands behind their backs. The sound of gunfire had gone silent. He wondered if any of the Red Wa soldiers were still alive.

They marched him and Arinya toward the site, illuminated by a faint red glow. A gigantic helicopter clattered by overhead and circled. The soldiers ushered them onto familiar ground, the place Kit had spent much of the last year digging. A bustle of activity surrounded a large plastic-wrapped block that could only be a hastily-excavated dinosaur skeleton.

In front of the skeleton, with their backs to him, were two women he recognized immediately despite the darkness and their masks: one dark-haired and tall, the other short and blonde. "Samira!" he shouted. "Beth!"

They both turned. Samira tore off her mask, her mouth dropping open in astonishment. "Kit?"

Arinya didn't hesitate. "Tell them to release us," she commanded.

"Sergeant, release these two," Samira said. "They're our friends."

"They drove in with the force that just assaulted us, ma'am," the soldier replied. "We'll keep them restrained until we're off the ground."

"They don't answer to me," Samira said to Arinya, almost desperately apologetic. "I'm not in charge, I'm just along for the ride."

Kit hated to see Samira manipulated like this. It was unquestionably the drug at work. Samira had never been this acquiescent and deferential in her life. But he wasn't going to ask Arinya to stop, either. Samira had infiltrated his country with an armed force to steal his fossils. She deserved what was coming to her.

"Make them," Arinya said.

"That's about enough out of you," the soldier said, but he was too late. Samira snatched his gas mask and pulled it down. His astonished intake of breath was all it took.

"Release us," Arinya said. "Give me your weapons."

"Whoa, what are you doing?" Beth asked, her mask still in place. The soldier ignored her. He cut Arinya and Kit's bonds and handed her his rifle, service pistol, and knife.

Arinya pointed the pistol at Beth. "Take your mask off," she said.

"Don't shoot her," Kit said. "She's my friend, you don't need to shoot her." He found it hard to protest with conviction, though. Arinya's scent affected him as well, and although she had given him no direct orders, it took effort even to object to her actions.

"I won't shoot her if she takes off the mask," Arinya said.

"Take it off, Beth," Samira said.

Beth looked at her, incredulous. "What's wrong with you? I don't understand what's happening here."

Arinya raised the pistol and cocked the hammer. "It's simple. Lose the mask, now. I won't ask again."

Kit stepped forward, putting his body between Beth and the pistol, and yanked off her mask. "There," he said. "It's done. No shooting needed."

Arinya scowled at him, but before she could say anything, the rest of the special ops team had noticed what was going on and trained their weapons on Arinya. "Stand in front of me," she told the soldier she'd unmasked, and he did as instructed.

"What's your name?" she asked.

"Sergeant Peter Weissman, ma'am."

"Well, Peter, you stand right there, and if they start shooting, you block the bullets, okay?"

"Yes, ma'am."

Arinya pointed the gun at the back of Sergeant Weissman's head. She raised her voice. "Drop your weapons, or I will shoot your friend."

The soldiers didn't move. "What do you want?" asked one of them. The soldiers wore no name tags or insignia of rank, but this one seemed to be their leader.

"I want you to leave our country without taking anything from this site."

"Not going to happen," the leader said. "I have a counter-offer for you. Walk away now, and we'll leave you alive."

Arinya lowered her voice. "What happened to the men we came with?" she asked Weissman.

"Most of them are dead," he replied through gritted teeth. "The rest fled."

Kit knew better than to expect the survivors would circle around and rejoin the fight. Arinya would know it, too. They were drug runners, not soldiers. They were used to the overwhelming odds being in their own favor. It was just Arinya and Kit now against a company of highly trained American special forces.

Or, he supposed, it was just Arinya against the Americans. It wasn't like Kit had any more choice in the matter than Samira or Beth did.

CHAPTER TWENTY-FOUR

Samira knew exactly what was happening to her. She had seen Sergeant Bowman unable to avoid the electric shocks to his stomach. The idea of someone having that kind of power over someone else had been scary then. Now it was utterly terrifying.

Knowing what was happening didn't help at all. The Thai woman with Kit was half her size, and until a moment ago, had her hands tied behind her back. But when she told Samira to do something, Samira had no choice but to obey. It wasn't just explicit commands, either; she couldn't resist her at all. It was as if Samira knew, bone-deep, that the woman had authority and power over her, and that nothing she could do could change that.

"Walk away now, and we'll leave you alive," Gutierrez called. When the Thai woman didn't respond, he said, "There's no way out of this for you. I know how you're controlling them, and my men and I will not remove our masks. If you approach, we will shoot you. If you open fire, my men and I will kill you and take what we came for anyway. Your only choice is to walk away."

"I could have your own people attack you," the Thai

woman shouted. "They would do it. You'd have to shoot them down yourself."

"And you would still die, and we would still finish our mission," Gutierrez said. He sounded calm and reasonable. Samira didn't know how he kept his cool. "If you surrender, we won't harm you."

"Why would I believe that? You fired on us first. You killed our men."

"They were armed. We could have killed you, too, but we took you captive instead. We would have left you here, unharmed. We still will if you drop your weapons and allow our people to put their masks back on."

"You're in our country illegally!" the woman shouted, getting more agitated. "You came here to steal and you killed our people! I don't trust you for a moment!"

"Wait!" Samira shouted. She took a step forward, waving her arms. She found that as long as her intentions were to save this Thai woman's life, she could act. "Everybody calm down. There's a solution to this that doesn't involve any more killing."

"Get back here," the Thai woman growled. Samira obeyed instantly.

"What are you talking about?" the woman asked.

"The block we pulled out of the stone is made of the green substance that everyone is fighting over," she said. "It's that substance that you want, right?"

The woman nodded. "And that's what you came to steal."

Samira raised her voice to make sure Gutierrez could hear her. "Captain, that block has been sweating liquid ever since we exposed it to the air. There's got to be a gallon of it at the bottom of the plastic."

"What's your point?" Gutierrez called out.

"Poke a hole," Samira said. "Drain it out into a container or two and leave it here for them. We take the fossil, they get the chemical they need."

The Thai woman shoved the rifle in Samira's face. "All of it is ours. You Americans think the world belongs to you, but it doesn't. You're not leaving here with our property."

"Your personal property?" Samira asked. "Or do you speak for the country as a whole? Because last time I checked, your government awarded the contents of this site to my team, a privilege for which we paid a significant sum."

The woman straightened her back. "My name is Dr. Arinya Tavaranan. I represent Princess Sirindhorn of the royal family, who speaks for this country more than the corrupt government that signed your contract."

Samira stared down the barrel of the rifle into the woman's face. She wanted to give in just to please her. She wanted to give her everything she had. But she also knew there would be bloodshed on both sides unless they could strike a deal. "They're going to kill you," she said softly. "They'll complete their mission at any cost. If you or I or even a few of them die to make that happen, they'll do it. Take what you can get."

Arinya was silent for a moment. Then she shouted across to Gutierrez, "Give me the liquid first, and then I will release your friends."

"No deal," Gutierrez said. "I'm leaving with what I came for. You can decide whether to leave or die trying to stop me."

"Captain, please," Samira said. "It's a fair trade. A bit of chemical for the lives of three people."

"If this chemical gets into Chinese hands, it'll be a lot more than three people dead," Gutierrez said.

Kit suddenly spoke up. "We won't give it to the Chinese. We just want it to protect ourselves. To keep the Chinese out."

"And the Americans," Arinya added, unhelpfully.

"Trust me, Captain," Samira said. "It's the fossil you want. You brought me for my scientific expertise, and I'm telling you, let this go. The chemical is expendable. The fossil we can study and understand. Now let's do this and get out of here while we still can."

The two sides stared at each other across the field for a while, neither backing down. Then Gutierrez said, "Fine. We'll make the trade." He lifted his radio. "Stallion One, we are ready for lift."

The huge helicopter circled back to hover over the site. Cables dropped from it, and soldiers gathered around to attach them to the block.

Arinya looked at Samira. "Go get me what you promised," she said. "Use any means you have to."

Eager to please, Samira ran towards the site, only to be stopped by soldiers with weapons drawn. "Sorry," Gutierrez said. "I know how this works. We can't trust you now."

"She told me to get what we promised her."

Gutierrez nodded to one of the soldiers. "Escort her. Treat her like a captive enemy combatant. She gathers the chemical and returns, nothing else."

The soldier nodded and followed her, his service pistol in his hand.

Men pulled on cables and shouted to each other over the roar of the helicopter, trying to attach the cables to the plastic-wrapped block. Samira took four one-quart canteens and dumped out the water. She knelt near a bulge in the plastic where liquid had gathered. "I need a hole, right here," she said. The soldier took out his knife and punched a tear in the plastic. A cloying gasoline smell drifted up as a thick, green liquid ran into the canteen.

The rich smell filled her nostrils. She took a deep breath through her mouth, trying to clear her head, when suddenly she saw the impossible. A feathered maniraptor loomed over her, cocking its head. Samira screamed and fell backwards, shielding her face. The soldier escorting her looked startled, but at her reaction, not at the dinosaur that had materialized in front of them. It was right there! Couldn't he see it?

As she scrambled backward, the soldiers, the plastic-wrapped block, the helicopter, and the rest of the Kalasin night faded away. She found herself in an interior space she'd never seen before, but that somehow felt very familiar...

EASY PREY TRIED TO CONCENTRATE, but the music made it hard. The sweet-smelling love songs his coworkers preferred left an acid taste in the back of his throat. He would have used a portable facemask for his own music—Prey liked his songs pungent, with a little more rhythmic savagery in them—but Sharp Salt, his boss, had strictly forbidden personal music organisms. Ruins team unity, she said.

SHE WAS THERE. Samira *was* Easy Prey. She remembered being dominated by Sharp Salt, remembered discovering the asteroid as if she had done it herself, and then using a connected network of fellow maniraptors to confirm its course and trajectory. She felt the horror of realizing its ultimate destination.

It seemed like hours, but when she finally opened her eyes, the soldier escorting her had barely moved. He had taken a step back and raised his pistol slightly, but everything else was just as it had been.

"Are you all right?" the soldier asked.

"I'm fine, I think. She sat up and checked the canteen. It hadn't even overflowed. She switched it out for the next and twisted the cap shut.

What had just happened? The liquid must be a hallucinogen of some kind, but not like anything she'd ever heard of. It had acted so quickly, not like a high or a dream state, but like an experience injected directly into her brain. She could still remember it vividly, as if she herself had been Easy Prey. Was it possible? Could this be a true recording of the thoughts of an intelligent creature that had lived millions of years ago?

Not only that, the experience had cleared the compulsion she'd felt to obey Arinya's instructions, or else the effect had faded with distance and time. Samira finished filling the four quart bottles anyway. Arinya still held Beth captive, and now that Samira was no longer under her thrall, the emotions of fear and fury came crashing in. Who was Arinya working for? Was Kit actually willing to threaten his friends and coworkers with death? Or was he under her sway as well?

It didn't matter. The best chance to get Beth back safe was to give her what she wanted. Maybe that meant more people would have their minds enslaved; she didn't know. But she had to get Beth back.

"I need a mask," she told the soldier guarding her.

Still looking at her suspiciously, he pulled a spare off of his belt and tossed it to her. She lowered it over her face and tightened the strap in back. Then she picked up the canteens and headed back the way she had come, past the soldiers whose rifles were still trained on Arinya and Kit and their captives.

Samira stopped halfway and set the full canteens on the ground. "I brought what you asked for," she called. "Now let them go."

Arinya held her gaze for a moment. "Okay," she said. "I'm trusting you." She looked at Beth and then at the soldier. "Go ahead."

Beth and Sergeant Weissman ran back toward Samira.

"Kit?" Samira said. "What about you? Are you okay?"

"You shouldn't be here, Samira," he said.

"Is she controlling you?" she asked, not sure if Kit could answer honestly or not.

"Arinya's a good person," he said. "She's not the one invading someone else's country." He paused, then nodded at the canteens. "Did you smell it?"

Samira nodded, still feeling awed by the experience.

"It's real," he said. "I matched up the stars. It really happened."

"How can that be?"

"They had a technology founded on chemicals and genetics that developed from their sense of smell. This site was a hibernation chamber, to survive the asteroid. They knew the asteroid was coming, Samira. They were preparing for it. That liquid is their cultural memory; their history, stored for future generations."

"You've discovered a lot."

"And we'd discover more, if you'd leave us alone. You shouldn't be here."

She could see things from his perspective, suddenly: Americans and Chinese both pushing their way into his country and taking what they wanted, using their guns if their money wasn't enough. "I'm sorry," she said.

"Just go."

Gutierrez's voice boomed over the sound of the helicopter. "Move out! We've got more company on the way. This is not a drill, people."

The plastic-wrapped fossil rose up in the air, drawn by its cables toward the massive helicopter. Two chain ladders dropped, twisting in the air. Soldiers grabbed the bottom rungs and began to scramble up with athletic speed.

More company? Did that mean more enemy soldiers? Samira thought she didn't have any adrenaline left in her body, but another shot of it set her heart pounding and put her nerves on edge. She let herself be ushered forward to the ladder and hauled herself upward. The ladder swung crazily. Her hair was whipped by the wind from the helicopter's rotors. With a deep breath, she climbed higher, ignoring the drop until men from above seized her arms and lifted her on board.

The rest of the soldiers climbed on with impressive speed, leaving most of their gear behind. They secured the fossil as the helicopter gained altitude and turned back the way it had come. Samira watched Kit dwindle into the distance, wondering if she would ever see him again.

Sergeant Weissman came up behind her. "Thank you," he said. "You saved my life."

"It was terrifying," she said. "I wasn't just *forced* to obey her. I *wanted* to. Everson was right. That drug is the most terrifying weapon I've ever seen."

"What's scary is that our enemies already have it," Weissman said.

"What's scary is that *anyone* has it. It should be destroyed."

Weissman nodded. "At least what we left behind will be."

"What do you mean?"

"We wired the site with explosives. As soon as we're clear, the captain will give the order and we'll blow it. There won't be anything left for anyone else to find."

Samira lurched and nearly fell out of the helicopter. "What? You can't do that! That's my friend down there. He's a scientist, not a soldier."

Weissman looked skeptical. "He seems to have picked a side. And it isn't ours."

"But we made a deal."

Weissman shook his head. "You saw what that stuff can do. We can't let any more get into enemy hands."

Samira looked back out towards the site, but she couldn't see Kit anymore.

CHAPTER TWENTY-FIVE

K it and Arinya watched the helicopter go. A faint light brightened the sky to the east. It was almost dawn.

"Get the canteens," Arinya said. "We'll take them back to Mai. Then we'll have to come again with a larger force and secure this area permanently. There are a lot more skeletons in the ground yet, which means a lot more of the memory liquid."

"What's that sound?" Kit asked. A rumbling in the distance grew steadily louder.

"Vehicles," Arinya said. "Heading this way. Hurry, let's get out of here."

The truck they'd come in had one of its front tires blown out, but it was the best shot they had. They could have run back the way they'd come, looking for the other Red Wa vehicles, but their tires had likely all been shot as well, and they would have had to contend with the bodies. Better to make do with what they had.

Kit jumped into the passenger seat, brushing pebbled windshield glass out of his way, and Arinya took the driver's seat. She turned the engine on, and they lurched forward, the flat tire flapping and pulling them to the right. It didn't matter. They just had to make it to Khai Nun, where they could commandeer a working vehicle to get them back to Tachileik.

They didn't make it.

The approaching engine noises increased to a roar, and three military trucks appeared, kicking up dust as they advanced at high speed. Two of them had giant tripod-mounted machine guns on top. The trucks stopped right in front of the site. Soldiers in the uniform of the Royal Thai Army poured out and spilled over the dig like ants.

At first, Kit thought the soldiers must not have seen them, but then one of the machine guns swiveled toward their limping truck. "Step out of the vehicle," a voice instructed them over a megaphone. "Keep your hands where we can see them."

Kit recognized that voice. It was the colonel.

"I don't have any more of the chemical," Arinya said, panicked. "I used the last of it."

Kit lifted one of the quart bottles. "We've got these. Could you—"

She gave an incredulous cough. "Sure, with a lab and a day to work on it."

"Step out of the vehicle," the voice insisted.

They had no choice. Kit and Arinya stepped out, their hands held high.

The passenger door of one of the trucks opened, and the colonel stepped out. His glaringly white uniform shone and his glasses reflected the rising sun. He wore a uniform cap to protect his bald head. Kit felt a rush of fear.

The colonel took his time, picking his way over the uneven ground before stopping well short of their position. Two soldiers flanked him, their rifles pointed at Kit and Arinya.

"Explain," the colonel said.

"An American special ops team flew in and stole our fossils," Kit said, speaking too fast.

"You are working with them?" the colonel asked. He might as well have been asking about the weather forecast, but Kit was certain he was moments away from telling his soldiers to shoot them both.

"No!" Kit said. "We didn't know they would be here. They held us back at gunpoint. We thought they might kill us."

"How did they know about this site?"

"The American scientists. Two of them were here, helping the soldiers."

The colonel's face tightened and turned red. "I should have held them," he said. "That fool at State Security ordered me to release them, to not *create a diplomatic incident*. Now look what's happened."

"There are more fossils there," Kit said. "We could get back to work. There's a lot more to learn."

He didn't want to work for the colonel again, but he didn't think the colonel would just let them drive away. Either they appeared to be on his side, or they would be taken into custody or just shot and left out here on the barren plateau.

The colonel scowled. "Last time you worked for me, I found all my men dead and the two of you missing. Now here you are, and my fossils are being carted off by American soldiers. There are at least a dozen dead bodies on the road half a kilometer from here, I want to know *what happened*."

"Oh, it was awful!" Arinya said, a desperate tremor in her voice. Kit looked over in surprise to see that she was actually crying. "It was the Red Wa. They kidnapped us. They tied me down and then they… they…" She burst into sobbing so real Kit wanted to put an arm around her to comfort her.

The colonel seemed much less moved. "Then how did you get here?"

"They forced us," she said. "They wanted the fossils, too. Then the Americans attacked, and there were bullets everywhere, and blood, and screaming. Our only thought was to get away."

He eyed her, suspicious. "You will both come with me," he said. "There will be no more disappearing. There will be no more communication with outsiders. You will dig this site, and you will do exactly as I say, and you will be watched."

A commotion at the site caught the colonel's attention and he turned around. "It's wired!" a soldier shouted, running away as fast as he could. "Clear the site!" It's—"

The explosion tore the world away. A shriek of light and sound ripped the ground from under Kit's feet. The shock wave pummeled him, and for a moment, he thought he was on fire. A sound like a hailstorm followed, rocks falling from the sky to strike his legs, his stomach, his face. When the rocks stopped falling, he sucked in a scalding breath and nearly choked on the suffocating petroleum odor.

A maniraptor loomed above him, then another, and another, and another, bringing with them that familiar sense of terror. He tried to scramble away, but his body didn't seem to be responding. Then the memories began.

There were memories of everyday life: affection and hatred, kindness and injustice, petty squabbles and unexpected good fortune. Some were surprisingly human; others alien and bizarre. They compounded on one another, until Kit felt like he was living a dozen lives at once. Then came the cataclysm: fear and death and impending extinction. He experienced the race to the modification pits from a dozen perspectives. He saw murder and backstabbing along with moments of incredible self-sacrifice. The memories piled on top of each other, like watching every TV channel at once, until he couldn't remember who he was.

Then they stopped. His eyes fluttered open. Dust billowed around him, and he panicked, thinking the asteroid was coming. His feathers were covered with dirt and pebbles, but when he lifted his arms... he realized he didn't have feathers. He was human. His name was Kit. He lived in Thailand, and the greatest fossil find in the history of the world had just been blown up by American soldiers.

He dragged himself up onto shaky legs and got his balance. The world around him was still except for the swirling dust. Arinya lay beside him, blood covering half of her face. Her eyes opened, focused, locked on him. "Arinya," he said, to help her remember. She shifted, trying to sit up. He reached down to give her a hand, but she slapped him away and scrambled to her feet.

"What happened to the others?" she asked.

No one else was moving. They walked to where the colonel had been standing. The soldiers flanking him lay still, lifeless. The colonel himself sprawled awkwardly, one leg badly turned underneath a large rock. His eyes flitted back and forth, unfocused.

"Let's get out of here," Kit said.

Arinya didn't answer. She lifted a rifle from one of the soldiers and pulled back the slide. She aimed at the colonel's head.

"No," Kit said. "Please, Arinya, enough killing. Let's go back to Mai."

Arinya stood there, her face a mask, one finger on the trigger.

"Come on," Kit said again.

Finally, her muscles loosened, and she lowered the weapon.

He reached out to take her hand, then thought better of it. "Let's go," he said again.

She followed him back to the damaged truck. He started the engine, and they jolted their way along the road toward Khai Nun.

THE DAY after Mai surrendered to the Red Wa army, its leaders proclaimed her senior general in command of the Wa State forces. The Wa State already had a senior general at their headquarters in Pangkham, but that didn't matter. When Pangkham sent more forces, Mai surrendered to them as well, only to emerge again with the same rank and a larger army. She only had to dominate those at the top, since everyone else in the hierarchy followed their orders. By the time three weeks had passed, Mai controlled all of Wa State, thirty thousand soldiers strong, as well as its multi-billion dollar business in illegal goods.

Kit remained at her side, more devoted to her with each passing day. She was demolishing the largest drug and sex trafficking organization in Asia and at the same time building her own private army. Was there anything she couldn't do?

He checked the news regularly, which showed General Wattana consolidating his power in Thailand. His ties to China became more evident with each new day. The man had murdered the royal family, Kit was sure of it, and yet he continued to rule the country without significant opposition. Any major government figures who could have opposed him were now dead or in exile.

"We are a modern country," Wattana said in a national address, "ready to set aside old-fashioned ideas and take our place on the world stage. We have no need of a king."

Kit looked over at Mai, who at that moment stood tall and regal on a pedestal in front of Tachileik's golden pagoda, surrounded by a crowd of followers who chanted her name as Buddhist monks draped strings of flowers around her neck.

Perhaps not, he thought. *Perhaps what we need is a queen.*

CHAPTER TWENTY-SIX

"It's about time," Samira said.

"Be nice," Beth said. "They're letting us in. Don't make them reconsider."

They had finally returned to the underground facility in the mountains. Everson handed them both badges and led them to the elevator.

"I've been calling you for months," Samira said. "You've completely ignored me."

"I'd still be ignoring you if it were up to me," Everson said. "A very persistent friend of yours pushed my superiors on it until they overruled me."

"You keep referring to this person," Samira said. "I don't know anyone in the CIA except for you. How is it that I have a mysterious benefactor who outranks you?"

"They don't outrank me," Everson said with a sour expression. "They just never shut up about you."

They took the red elevator down to the twelfth floor, the deepest underground. Besides using his badge, Everson had to enter a code on a numeric keypad before the doors would open.

"You're not going to tell us who it is?"

"You'll find out soon enough."

The elevator doors opened and they followed him down a hallway. They stopped at a metal door that looked like the outside of a vault.

"We're going in there?" Beth asked.

"Not quite yet." He led them into a side room and closed the door. The new room had a metal table with five chairs, and nothing else. One entire wall of the room was mirrored. He indicated the two seats facing the mirror, and Samira and Beth sat. Samira felt like a suspect being interrogated in a police movie. She wondered if someone was watching them from the other side of the mirrored glass.

"What are we doing?" she asked.

"Just dotting a few i's," Everson said. His assistant, Michelle Jiankui, came in with a briefcase and sat, laying it on the table. She lifted two packets of paper out of the briefcase and passed them across to Samira and Beth. "Can you verify that this is your security paperwork, for the record?" Her tone was brusque and businesslike.

"What is this?" Samira demanded. "I nearly get killed helping you retrieve a valuable fossil, then you don't answer my calls for three months, and now you want to do security paperwork?"

"Please," Everson said.

Samira glanced through it. "Yes, that's mine."

"Beth?"

She nodded.

"Out loud, please."

"Yes."

"Samira and Bethany Shannon, do you swear, for the record and on pain of legal penalties to include imprisonment or death, that you will communicate nothing about what you see beyond this point to anyone outside this facility?" Michelle intoned.

"I agree," Beth said.

Samira looked around for the camera, feeling uneasy. "Yes, I agree, I won't tell anyone. Are you going to show us our fossil now?"

Everson folded his fingers together over the table. "In the room I'm about to take you, you may see things that are startling or even frightening, things that you don't understand, or that violate your own personal ethics. Again, for the record, do you willingly bind yourself to prosecution and/or imprisonment if you reveal what you see to another person?"

Beth gave a nervous laugh. "Are you trying to get us to change our mind?"

"Just answer the question please."

"Yes," Samira said. Beth nodded, and then remembered to say, "Yes."

Michelle smiled grimly. "Excellent. I'll just have you sign these, and we can continue on." She slid three more documents across the table to each of them.

Samira read quickly, but they seemed to be longer versions of what Everson had already said, and to which they both had already agreed. She signed.

Michelle filed the documents back into her case and went out the way she'd come. Everson led the way back to the vault door, which clicked and swung open as they approached it. Samira thought someone must certainly have been watching them through one-way glass, or at least listening in on their conversation, but when they entered, she saw no one on the other side.

THE FIRST DOOR featured a yellow biohazard warning sign and read, "DANGER. Biological test site. Risk of airborne pathogens and/or harmful biological agents. Use extreme caution."

"That's ominous," Beth said.

"I hope you've been taking good care of that fossil," Samira said. "Something that well-preserved, it's going to be extremely fragile. Simple contact with the air can cause it to deteriorate."

"You're not the only expert in this facility," Everson said. "I don't think you'll have any complaints how well-preserved your fossil has been."

The badge reader clicked and turned green at Everson's card, and when he entered the correct number sequence, the door unlocked with the thunk of magnetic bolts disengaging. As he pushed against it, air whistled around the edges and a breeze ruffled her hair. Positive air pressure to keep out contaminants.

They entered a small, windowless room like an airlock. The door shut behind them with a solid click. After it closed, a light above the opposing door turned green, and Everson pulled it open, the breeze following them out this time.

The laboratory beyond didn't immediately strike Samira as unusual. She saw a glass-fronted refrigerator with metal racks inside, several tissue culture hoods, autoclaves, laptops, centrifuges, microscopes, the usual array of glassware. A DNA sequencer stood on a table, with a large mass spectrometer standing next to it on the floor. All the equipment looked new and high-quality, but not out of the ordinary. Half a dozen men and women looked up briefly as they entered, then returned to their work.

"What are they studying?" Samira asked.

"Your fossil," Everson said. "Though I'm not sure that's quite the right word for it,"

Everson walked across the room. Samira glanced at Beth, then they hurried after him. "What do you mean, it's not the right word?" Beth asked.

"Sorry to be vague," he said, "but there's really no explaining it. You have to see for yourself." He was enjoying himself, Samira realized. She wanted to throttle him.

They passed through another door and down a long hallway that descended slightly as they walked. The air felt warmer here and more humid, unusual for what until now had been a series of aggressively controlled environments.

Samira shivered. "Feels like a cave."

They passed through another door decorated with screaming biological warning signs and into another pressurized room. As the door shut, Everson indicated a row of yellow hazmat suits along the wall. "Pick out your favorite color," he said, "as long as it's yellow."

Samira stared at the suits, then at him. "Seriously?"

He shrugged. "No one goes beyond this point without one. We're almost there. Bear with me."

They suited up, allowing Everson to check the seals and air tank. Samira had never worn a hazmat suit before and felt the first signs of panic. Her breath felt hot in her face, and she felt like she wasn't getting enough air. Everson's voice sounded through a tinny speaker in her helmet. "Under no circumstances are you to take this off," he said. "Seriously. Even if you can't breathe, you get back to this room before you take off the helmet."

That didn't help. Samira didn't think of herself as excitable, but her heart was hammering in her chest.

"Are you okay?" Beth asked. Samira could hear her perfectly; there must be microphones and speakers connecting them.

She took a deep breath. "I think so. I wish Everson would tell us what's going on here, though. I'm starting to regret agreeing to this."

"Not a chance of that," Everson said. "Beyond this door is the scientific discovery of the age, perhaps of any age." He grinned. "Try not to scream."

He pulled open the door and held it, gesturing for them to enter first. The first thing she saw on the other side was someone waiting in another hazmat suit. A short, round woman whose suit seemed specially tailored for her size. The face beyond the clear plastic helmet panel was smiling.

"Paula?" Samira stepped forward with delight. Of course. This explained everything. *She* was the secret benefactor Everson kept mentioning. Paula Shapiro worked for the CIA. That it was her old mentor behind the scenes pulling those strings and asking for her by name made perfect sense.

Something clicked in Samira's mind just before she saw it. Biological hazard signs. 'Fossil' being the wrong word. An ancient hibernation chamber. *No.*

She stopped dead as she caught a glimpse of the thing behind Paula. An utterly impossible thing, moving with deadly speed and grace.

She screamed.

CHAPTER TWENTY-SEVEN

The first thing Prey smelled was himself. He reeked. He rarely went even a few hours without a bath, and judging by the odor, it had been days at least. He hoped no one else was around. As far as he could tell, though, there was no one nearby, not for miles.

He sifted the air through his nostrils. Strange. No one at all. He couldn't smell the city network, or any of the rural nodes, or...anything. No plants, no earth, no rain, no life at all. The oxygen content of the air was low, with a taste of carbon dioxide and a lot more nitrogen than he was used to. Where was he?

He opened his eyes.

THIS IS the end of Book 1 of the <u>Living Memory</u> series. Look for Book 2, <u>Deadly Memory,</u> coming in 2023!

OTHER BOOKS BY DAVID WALTON

The Genius Plague (Winner of the Campbell Award for Best SF
Novel of the Year)

Three Laws Lethal (Wall Street Journal Best of SF List 2019)

Terminal Mind (Winner of the Philip K. Dick Award)

Superposition

Supersymmetry

ACKNOWLEDGMENTS

Many thanks as always to the friends who read my books in their unpolished form and tell me everything I do wrong: Chad and Jill Wilson, David Cantine, Nadim Nakhleh, Mike Yeager, and Joe Reed. For this book, special thanks goes to Dr. Michael Brett-Surman, formerly Museum Specialist for Dinosaurs, Fossil Reptiles, and Amphibians at the National Museum of Natural History of the Smithsonian Institution. This book has many flights of fancy which are not his fault, but he reviewed an earlier draft and helped me get the real paleontology right. Thanks to Alex Shvartsman for publishing advice and ebook formatting. Finally, thanks to you, dear reader, for taking a chance on this book when you had so many other options available. I hope you enjoyed it!

ABOUT THE AUTHOR

David Walton is an aerospace engineer and the father of eight children. His love for dinosaurs started as a boy, but it wasn't until his own young son's enthusiasm that he really started to learn about how they lived and what they were like. His research obsessions have also included fungus (*The Genius Plague*), self-driving cars (*Three Laws Lethal*), and quantum physics (*Superposition*). When he's not writing, he's reading, playing piano, watching dinosaurs through his binoculars, or laughing with his family around the dinner table.

CPSIA information can be obtained
at www.ICGtesting.com
Printed in the USA
LVHW011934261022
731644LV00006B/130